"Have di..."

Her jaw clenched—he hadn't... as a question. "No." She gave the word all the finality she could muster.

"Because of the chair?"

"Not because of the chair, because we are currently working together on a school matter."

He leaned back. "It's because of the chair."

Heather planted her hands on the table. "It's because of the arrogant, pushy man *in* the chair." She let out a breath and began putting the notebook back into her handbag. "I was just trying to be nice, to celebrate all the good you've done with Simon, but I should have known it'd get like this. I'll walk back to school, thanks."

Max put his hands up. "Okay, okay. I'll take it down a notch. Let's have pie and coffee and talk about Simon, and I'll keep my dinner plans with Alex and JJ and pretend this never happened."

She glared at him. "You were going to ditch Alex and JJ for dinner?"

"Well, not really. I was pretty sure you'd say

...ut one hand to her forehead. "You are ...y impossible. You should come with a ...label."

Books by Allie Pleiter

Love Inspired

My So-Called Love Life
The Perfect Blend
*Bluegrass Hero
*Bluegrass Courtship
*Bluegrass Blessings
*Bluegrass Christmas
Easter Promises
*"Bluegrass Easter"
†Falling for the Fireman
†The Fireman's Homecoming
†The Firefighter's Match
†A Heart to Heal

Love Inspired Single Title

Bad Heiress Day
Queen Esther &
the Second Graders of Doom

*Kentucky Corners
†Gordon Falls

Love Inspired Historical

Masked by Moonlight
Mission of Hope
Yukon Wedding
Homefront Hero
Family Lessons
The Lawman's Oklahoma Sweetheart

ALLIE PLEITER

Enthusiastic but slightly untidy mother of two, RITA® Award finalist Allie Pleiter writes both fiction and nonfiction. An avid knitter and unreformed chocoholic, she spends her days writing books, drinking coffee and finding new ways to avoid housework. Allie gre[w] Connecticut, holds a BS in speech from Nort[hwestern] University and spent fifteen years in the field [of profes]sional fund-raising. She lives with her husb[and, chil]dren and a Havanese dog named Bella in th[e suburbs] of Chicago, Illinois.

A Heart to Heal

Allie Pleiter

HARLEQUIN® LOVE INSPIRED®

Recycling programs for this product may not exist in your area.

™ LOVE INSPIRED BOOKS

ISBN-13: 978-0-373-81782-5

A HEART TO HEAL

www.Harlequin.com

Printed in U.S.A.

the deck and he smelled sour of sweat and his bad eye was swung wild again and all the plastic surgery on his face showed white. Thomas Hudson lay very quietly and listened to him.

"They had two burp guns only but they were set up good. Gil's first extinguisher got them and the .50's cut the shit out of them. Antonio hit them too. Henry can really shoot the .50's."

"He always could."

"I mean with the heat on. So we detrapped that joint and it is very high now. Ara and I cut all the wires but we left the stuff. She's OK and I'll pinpoint the location of these other Krauts on the chart."

The anchor was up and the motors were turning.

"We didn't do so good, did we?" Thomas Hudson said.

"They outsmarted us. But we had the firepower. They didn't do so good either. Don't say anything to Ara about the prisoner. He feels bad enough. He says he squeezed off before he thought."

The ship was heading toward the blue hills and gathering speed.

"Tommy," Willie said. "I love you, you son of a bitch, and don't die."

Thomas Hudson looked at him without moving his head.

"Try and understand if it isn't too hard."

Thomas Hudson looked at him. He felt far away now and there were no problems at all. He felt the ship gathering her speed and the lovely throb of her engines against his shoulder blades which rested hard against the boards. He looked up and there was the sky that he had always loved and he looked across the great lagoon that he was quite sure, now, he would never paint and he eased his position a little to lessen the pain. The engines were around three thousand now, he thought, and they came through the deck and into him.

"I think I understand, Willie," he said.

"Oh shit," Willie said. "You never understand anybody that loves you."

THE END

The light shines in the darkness,
and the darkness has not overcome it.
—*John* 1:5

To Jeff
And he knows why

Acknowledgments

Some stories beg relentlessly to be told,
even if it poses a challenge. My thanks to
Erin Kinahan for sharing her experience of life in a
wheelchair with me, and for the ongoing assistance
of Dr. David Chen from the Rehabilitation Institute
of Chicago for his medical expertise. I also owe a
debt of thanks to author and wheelchair rugby star
Mark Zupan for his frank and compelling memoir,
Gimp, which helped me to understand Max's
experience. If any of the medical or disability facts
of this book are incorrect, the fault lies with me and
not with any of these generous experts.

Chapter One

High school guidance counselor Heather Browning was twenty minutes into The Backup Plan and regretting it already.

Principal Margot Thomas seemed to agree. "That's who you called to help Simon?"

Simon Williams, the frail but brilliant freshman boy who was Heather's biggest concern this year, had already become the target of a senior thug. "It's still August. We're two days into the school year," Heather admitted. "I thought I'd have more time than this to get Simon settled before anyone bothered him." But that wasn't the way it had turned out. Her initial goal—help Simon find some friends who would be protective camouflage against getting noticed by bullies—hadn't worked fast enough.

The principal looked out the school window at that "backup plan" as he appeared in the parking lot. A boxy black car with flames painted on the side pulled into the handicapped-accessible parking space. Max Jones had arrived.

"This afternoon at lunch, Jason Kikowitz decided Simon was sitting too close to the 'varsity table.' Evidently he grabbed the back of Simon's wheelchair and spun him around, knocking most of Simon's books out of his backpack."

"Sounds like our Kikowitz," Margot commiserated. "I'll be glad when that boy graduates—*if* he graduates."

"Simon spun around fast enough to whack Jason in the shins with the footrest of his wheelchair. It must've hurt, because evidently Jason hopped around on one foot and swore a blue streak in front of the lunch monitor."

Margot gave the sigh of the weary. "Lovely."

"At least it gave Simon a chance to get away. For now. You know Kikowitz," Heather explained, feeling less and less sure of her course of action. "He's likely to lay into Simon every day this week, even if I give him twenty detentions."

The older woman looked at Heather with determination in her eyes. "You know I'll back you up on those even if Coach Mullen gives me grief."

Heather was grateful for Margot Thomas every single day. The principal was an outstanding administrator who cared enough to address problems head-on, even when it meant things got sticky. "Thanks, but you and I both know detentions don't stop Kikowitz. What we need is help for Simon, and the assistance agency couldn't come through with a proper mentor until next month. We don't have that long, so I called JJ." JJ was Heather's friend and Max's sister. And Max Jones, or "Hot Wheels," as a local magazine had dubbed him during their coverage of his highly publicized injury and recovery, was quite possibly the last thing Simon Williams needed. Even if he was the only other resident of Gordon Falls who used a wheelchair, Max seemed to be everything Heather didn't want Simon to be rolled up into one defiant renegade.

The foolishness of calling on him struck her anew as she spied the HTWELZ2 license plate on the car. "Help me, Margot. I need wisdom and calm and I recruited a rolling tornado. Tell him I've been called into a meeting and that we don't need a mentor anymore. I've made a huge mistake, and I don't want Simon to pay for it."

Margot leaned back against the windowsill. "I won't tell him any such thing. I think I want to see how this turns out."

"I don't." Heather rested her forehead in her open hand.

Together Heather and Margot watched Max perform the complicated task of extracting his wheelchair—black with flames on it that matched his car—and settling himself into it. He was athletic, graceful even, and managed to look casual, as if the process were no more taxing than tying a shoe. He wore blue jeans, expensive sneakers and a gray T-shirt with the words *Ramp it up, baby* running across his chest. It was easy to see that his shoulders and biceps carried most of his weight—his arms were toned and outdoor tan. His large hands boasted black leather driving gloves, and his mussed dirty-blond hair framed a strong face. Heather thought he needed a shave, not to mention a haircut and probably half a dozen diplomacy lessons. "Honestly," she told her boss as Max started toward the ramp that led up the stairs to the school entrance, "that guy looks a far cry from an appropriate mentor for an impressionable teenager."

"He's a key executive at Adventure Access, which is supposed to be a fast-rising company in the adaptive recreation business. If they put faith in him," offered the principal, sounding as if she was grasping at straws and not a little bit amused, "maybe he's not as bad as…he looks."

"Oh, I expect he's worse," Heather moaned. JJ's husband, Alex Cushman, ran that fast-rising adaptive recreation company and had drafted Max as their spokesperson and development consultant. It wasn't hard to see why. Max Jones had been so handsome, daring, arrogant and flamboyant before he'd injured himself that he'd been chosen for a nationally televised reality television show featuring adventure sports. As cruel chance would have it, he'd gotten hurt on that TV show during a risky night climb. Yet looking at him now, it seemed as if his disability barely slowed him down.

"Simon will probably adore him," Margot offered.

"That's exactly what I'm afraid of," Heather moaned. "Nothing good can come from pairing that boy with that man."

Kids were not his thing. Not before, not now.

As he rolled up the ramp to the Gordon Falls High School entrance, Max had to wonder how he'd let JJ talk him into this. If the GFHS teachers knew the kind of tyrant he'd been in high school, they'd be barring the doors.

Only they wouldn't have to. Just take out the ramp and he couldn't get inside no matter how hard he tried. While he'd worked on the development of all kinds of adaptive gear in his new position at Adventure Access, even those top innovators hadn't yet come up with a wheelchair that could climb stairs.

Still, Max remembered the "special" kids from his high school days—not that long ago, for crying out loud—and how they'd been treated. It stuck in his gut that he'd been as mean as the next guy to kids who used wheelchairs or crutches or were in *those* classes. Max had done lots of crazy and regrettable things in high school, but those moments of picking on the weaker kids, the different kids—

those gnawed at him now. He'd only said yes to this stint as a "mentor" because JJ seemed to think it might make up for some of his past crimes.

It's four weeks with a gawky fifteen-year-old— I've faced far worse, Max assured himself as he punched the assistive-entrance button and listened to the door whoosh open in front of him. At least schools usually had all the adaptations right. He'd had to sit there feeling stupid the other week when a restaurant had to literally move four tables in order to let him sit down with JJ and have lunch. Then the server had asked JJ what her "special friend" would like to eat. The nerve of some people! He'd given the server such a loud piece of his mind that they'd comped his lunch just to get him out of the place.

He rolled into the entrance, marveling at how high school was still high school. The bang of lockers, the smattering of posters for dances and sporting events, the echo of shouts from a distant gymnasium—it all flung Max's mind back to those years. Hockey team. Prom. Working on his first car. Life was one big game back then, a never-ending stream of escapades, pranks and good times. He'd loved high school, been a master of the school scene— the social side of it, that was. Academics weren't ever his thing, though he'd managed to graduate just fine, despite a few…dozen…trips to the principal's office.

Funny that it was his first stop now—or rather,

the guidance counselor's office, which was practically the same thing.

"I'm Max Jones, here to see Heather Browning." Max swallowed his annoyance that he was calling toward a counter over which he could not see. Well over six feet when he could stand, he was especially annoyed by tall counters now that he navigated the world from about three feet lower.

A gray-haired lady—school secretaries evidently hadn't changed one bit since his varsity days popped up from behind the blue Formica to peer at him over the top of her glasses. "Mr. Jones?" She did the double take Max always enjoyed. Somehow people never expected to see a guy in a wheelchair looking like him, and he got a kick out of leveraging the "Hot Wheels" persona to challenge their assumptions.

Max flicked an Adventure Access business card up onto the counter—shiny black with flames along the bottom with his name and title, Company Spokesman and Adaptive Gear Development Specialist, screaming out in yellow letters. "In the flesh and on the roll."

Her wrinkled eyes popped wide for a moment, then narrowed in suspicion. "Is she expecting you?"

"Yes, I am" came a female voice from behind Max.

Max spun around and sucked in a breath. The high school guidance counselors he remembered didn't look like *that*. Maybe this wouldn't be such a rough gig after all. "Well, hello, Ms. Browning." He didn't even try to hide the pleasant surprise in his voice. Where had JJ been hiding this "friend"? If he'd had a counselor like Heather Browning trying to lure him into higher education, he'd be working on his PhD by now. She had fantastic hair—long, honey-colored curls tumbled down to her shoulders in a wave. Bottle-green eyes that—well, okay, they were currently scowling a bit at him, but he could handle that. People scowled at him all the time, and he much preferred it to the diverted glances of pity that some people threw him. Pulling off his driving glove, Max extended a hand. "I am most definitely pleased to meet you."

"Thanks for coming." He could tell she only barely meant it. He probably shouldn't have squealed his tires pulling into the parking lot like that.

"Anything for JJ," Max said as they went into her office. It was filled with all the stuff one would expect of a helping professional—inspirational quotes, pretty pictures, plants and pottery. The only surprising thing was a "flock" of various flamingo figurines on her bookshelf and a metal flamingo statue-ish thingy on her desk. Max picked it up and inspected it. "I'm surprised we haven't met before."

Ms. Browning plucked the metal bird from his hands, returned it to its perch on her desk and sat down. She crossed her arms. "We have. This summer at the church picnic."

He remembered that picnic as a rather boring affair, all happy community fried chicken and potato salad. Nice, if you liked that sort of thing, which he didn't.

"Mr. Jones, if you—"

"Max," he corrected.

"Max," she relented. "I want to state one thing right off. This is a serious time commitment, and I'm sure you're very busy. If you don't have the time to give Simon the attention he needs, I'll completely understand."

"Hang on." Max felt his stomach tighten at the low expectation expressed in her words. "I'm willing to make the time. Only I'm not really sure how you go about making freshman year of high school *not* hard, if you know what I mean. That's sort of how it goes, isn't it?"

"I'd like to think we can do better than that. A senior boy—Jason Kikowitz—has made Simon a target of sorts, and it's going to take more than a stack of detention slips to set things right."

"Kikowitz?" Max chuckled; the name brought up an instant vision of a thick-necked linebacker with a crew cut and four like-size friends. "Why do the thugs always have names like Kikowitz?"

She didn't seem to appreciate his commentary.

"I want Simon to learn the right way to stand up for himself while I get Mr. Kikowitz to change his thinking."

"Only Simon can't stand up for himself, can he? Wheelchair. That's the whole problem, isn't it?" People always talked around the wheelchair—the elephant in the room—and Max liked to make them face it outright. It made everything easier after that, even if it took an off-color joke to get there.

She flushed and broke eye contact. "It's part of the problem, yes."

"It's lots of the problem, I'd guess. Look, I'm in a chair. I get that. It's part of who I am now, and pretending I'm just like you isn't going to help anyone. It doesn't bug me, so don't let it bug you. I can take you out dancing if I wanted to, so I should be able to help this Simon kid hold his own."

"You cannot take me out dancing."

It was clear she wasn't the type to like a joke. "Well, not in the usual sense, but there's a guy in Chicago building an exoskeleton thingy that—"

"This is not a social meeting. Are we clear?"

She really did know how to suck all the fun out of a room.

"Crystal clear, Ms. Browning." She was too stiff to even match his invitation to use first names. He'd have to work on that. "What is it, exactly, that you think Simon needs?"

"Well, I'd have to say social confidence. He's led

a fairly sheltered life because of his condition, but he's brilliant…"

"The geeks always are."

She sat back in her chair. "Can you at least *try* to do this on a professional level?"

Max made a show of folding his hands obediently in his lap. "Okay, Counselor Browning. Simon needs some base-level social skills and maybe enough confidence to know high school is survivable. Have I got it?"

She seemed to appreciate that. "Yes, in a manner of speaking."

"And you're thinking you need something just a little out of the ordinary to solve the problem, right?"

"Well, I…"

"Hey, you called me, not the nice bland people from social services."

That probably wasn't a smart crack to make to someone in guidance counseling. Her eyes narrowed. "Yes, well, the nice, *appropriate* people from social services were not available. This isn't how I normally operate. It's only fair to tell you you're not my first choice."

Max could only smile. "Alternative. Well, I'd have to say that's exactly my specialty."

Chapter Two

Max hadn't really expected Appropriate Ms. Browning to go for the idea of a pickup basketball game—especially one with the twist he had in mind—but she surprised him by agreeing to book the school auxiliary gym. Two days later, Max found himself whistling as his basketball made a perfect arc, rolled dramatically around the rim and then settled obediently through the net. "Jones nails it from behind the line with seconds to spare."

His sister, JJ, palmed a ball against one hip. "Nice shot."

Max turned to face her. "Let me see you do one."

JJ nodded and dribbled the ball, getting ready to best her little brother. "No," Max corrected. "From the chair." He pointed toward the three armless, low-backed sports wheelchairs that sat against the wall. He'd decided even before he was out of the parking lot the other day that the best way to meet

Simon Williams was a pickup game of wheelchair basketball. The boys-against-girls element, with he and Simon facing JJ and Heather Browning? Well, that had been a brilliant afterthought.

JJ paused for a moment, shot Max the look years of sibling rivalry had perfected and sauntered over to the chair. After settling in, she wheeled toward him in a wobbly line, smirking. "Not so hard."

"Really?" Max teased, rocking back to pop a wheelie in his chair. "I've been waiting to smoke you on the court for months."

She laughed, trying to bounce the ball until it got away from her. "Just like you smoked me on the ski slope?"

Max shot over to scoop up the ball and passed it back to her. "Worse. Okay, try a shot."

JJ missed by a mile. "This is going to be harder than I thought."

Max grabbed the ball, dribbled up to the basket and sunk another one in. "Actually, this is going to be a lot more fun than I thought. Me and Simon should wipe the floor with you *girls*."

"Simon *and I*" came Heather's voice from the gym door. "And don't get too confident. You will get a fair fight from us *ladies*."

Max groaned, JJ smirked and the kid who had to be Simon Williams had the good sense to look a little baffled by whatever he'd just gotten himself into. The boy was spindly thin and a bit pale. His glasses sat a little crooked on his face, and a 1970s haircut didn't help his overall lack of style. Still, his sharp blue eyes and goofy grin made him oddly likable.

Max caught the kid's eye and lamented, "Teacher types."

"Yeah." The boy's response was noncommittal and soft. He'd expected the boy's smile to widen, but it had all but disappeared.

Shy, skinny and unsure of himself—Max remembered the years when he used to eat kids like this for breakfast. It wasn't a comfortable memory. He wheeled over to Simon and pointed to the line of chairs. "Can you transfer into that sports chair by yourself? I guessed on your size but I think it's close enough." Heather had given him some basic medical info on Simon's cerebral palsy—a condition that mostly left his legs too unstable to support him for more than a few steps.

"Uh-huh." Again, a small voice lacking any stitch of confidence. Max began to wonder if the kid had ever played any sport, ever. He looked as if his family hardly let him outside in the sunshine. Max pretended to be adjusting his gloves while he watched Simon slowly maneuver from his larger daily chair to the smaller, lower sports chair. It was a relief to see that he could do it by himself. The kid's steps were gangly and poorly controlled, but while Max had met other cerebral palsy patients with very spastic movements all over their bodies, Simon's seemed to be confined to his legs. He had the upper-body control to have some fun in a sports chair, yet he looked as if he'd never seen one. If he'd never known speed, this chair would be a barrel of fun. Somehow, he doubted this kid had ever seen much fun.

Whose fault was that? His shy personality? Or overprotective parents? Well, that drought was going to end today. The thought of introducing the boy to agility sparked a faint foreign glow of satisfaction that caught Max up short.

JJ noticed his reaction. She raised an eyebrow in inquiry as Simon finished settling himself into his seat. "What?"

"I think I just got a bit of an Alex rush." Max knew he'd regret admitting that to his sister. His boss—Alex Cushman, JJ's husband—was always going on and on about the charge he got from taking people out of their comfort zones into new adventures.

"Not all about the new toys anymore?" Her tone was teasing, but JJ's eyes were warm. That girl was so stuck on her new husband it was like a nonstop valentine to be with either one of them.

"No, it's still about the new toys." Max popped another wheelie and executed a tight circle around his sister. He turned his attention back to Simon, now sitting next to a delightfully baffled Heather as the two of them explored the gear. "What do you think?"

"They're crooked," Simon offered in a sheepish voice as he pointed to the wheels. Unlike the straight-up-and-down wheels of his daily chair, this chair's wheels tilted toward the middle.

"Nah, they're *cambered.* Gives you stability and agility. You can turn fast on these. Try it."

Max watched as Simon, JJ and Heather made circles in their chairs. Slow, careful circles. Max growled and came up behind JJ to give her a hefty shove. She shot forward, yelping, and then managed to turn herself around in a respectably quick U-turn. "Cut that out, Max!"

"Quit being snails, the lot of you. These things are made for speed. Use 'em!" He angled up next to Simon, who looked as if someone needed to give him permission to keep breathing. "Race ya."

"Huh?"

"First one to the end of the gym and back gets ice cream."

Simon just looked at him. Who'd been keeping this poor kid under glass? Max chose to ignore the uncertainty written on the boy's face and pretend his silence was a bargaining tactic.

"Okay, then, two ice creams and you get a three-second lead," he conceded. Max allowed himself a sly wink at the guidance counselor. "Ms. Browning said she'd buy."

"I never…"

Simon started pushing on his wheels. Max whooped. "One…two…three!"

A sweaty, crazy hour later, Heather had fed every dollar bill and coin she had into the school vending machine as she, Max, JJ and Simon sat on the school's front steps eating ice cream.

"There's a whole basketball league," Max explained to Simon. "And hockey. I've even seen a ski team." She watched Max look Simon up and down. "You're kinda skinny for the hockey thing, but I saw the way you shot today. Wouldn't take long for you to hold your own pretty nicely on the court."

"You outshot *me,*" JJ offered, licking chocolate off her fingers.

"I've always had a chair." Simon said it as if it was a weak excuse. The embarrassed tone in his voice burrowed into Heather's heart and made her want to send Jason Kikowitz to Mars.

A red van pulled up, and Heather saw Brian Williams wave his hand out the driver's side window.

"My dad's here," Simon said, tossing his last wrapper into the trash bin and angling toward the wheelchair ramp. At the top of the incline, he paused. "Thanks, Mr. Jones. That was fun."

"Max," Max corrected, making a funny face. "Nobody calls me Mr. Jones. Want to go sailing next week?"

Heather watched Simon's response. His eyes lit

up for a moment, then darkened a bit as he heard the door click open and the *whrrr* of the lift extending out of his parents' van. "I don't think my folks would go for it." Simon's lack of optimism stung. Heather knew that despite his spot on the Gordon Falls Volunteer Fire Department—or maybe because of it—Simon's dad was a highly protective father. She'd had a highly protective dad herself— she'd had her own share of medical challenges in high school—but even she had reservations about how far Brian Williams went to keep his son away from any kind of risk.

Max had caught the boy's disappointment. He waved at the van. "They'll say yes. Can I come meet them?"

"Um…maybe next time," Simon said, quickly darting down the ramp.

"Hey, slow down there, Speedy!" Simon's dad called as the lift platform rattled onto the ground. "Watch that crack there or your wheel might get stuck. You've got to take your time on ramps, remember?"

Heather heard Max mutter a few unkind words under his breath. JJ got to her feet. "Speaking of speed, my shift starts in half an hour and I've got to run home first." She gave Heather a hug, then pecked her brother on the cheek and snatched up the sweatshirt she'd been sitting on. "Dinner still on for next Thursday?"

"You bet," Max said, still staring as Simon was swallowed up by the van's mechanism. His irritation jutted out in all directions, sharp and prickly. "Does he know how much he's holding Simon back?" Max nearly growled. "Have you talked to him about it?"

"Hey," she said. "Cut the dad a little slack here, will you?"

"You know what half of Simon's problem is?" Max jutted a finger at the van as it pulled away. "*That*. I was trying to figure out what made Simon such a walking ball of shy and I just got my answer."

Heather swallowed her own frustration. People were shy for lots of reasons, not just fatherly protectiveness. "So after two hours with the boy, you've got him all figured out? Is that it?"

"It doesn't take a PhD in counseling to figure out they keep that kid under lock and key. He's afraid of his own shadow, and somebody had to teach him that."

"Aren't you coming down awfully hard on someone you hardly even know?"

"Simon's not sick. Okay, his legs don't work so hot, but I get how that goes. He could be so much stronger than he is. He could be doing so much *more*."

It needed saying. "He's not you, Max. Not everyone needs to come at this full throttle." When that just made him frown, Heather tried a different tack. "What were you like in high school?"

"A whole lot different than that. Even as a freshman."

"I can imagine that."

Max shook out the mane of shaggy dirty-blond hair that gave him such a rugged look. He was tanned and muscular—the furthest thing imaginable from Simon's pale, thin features—with mischievous eyes and a smile Heather expected made girls swoon back in high school. She found his not-quite-yet-cleaned-up-bad-boy persona as infuriating as it was intriguing. Max Jones just didn't add up the way he ought to, and she didn't know what to do with that.

Max tossed an ice-cream wrapper into the trash bin with all the precision he'd shown on the basketball court. "Truth is," he said, his voice losing the edge it had held a moment ago, "I was a lot closer to the Kikowitzes of the world than to geeky kids like Simon." He shot Heather a guilty glance. "Let's just say I've shoved my share of kids into lockers. And, okay, I'm not especially proud of it, but I think I'd rather be that than go through life like Simon."

Heather tried to picture a teenage Max prowling the halls of GFHS, picking on kids and collecting detention slips. It didn't take much imagination. "Football team? Motorcycles?"

He laughed, and Heather reminded herself how

such charming smiles shouldn't always be trusted. Sometimes those dashing ways covered some pretty devastating weaknesses. "No," he corrected her. "Basketball and my dad's old Thunderbird. Well, before I rolled it my junior year, that is."

"You were a terror in high school." She nodded over to the black car with flames and the HTWELZ2 license plate. "It boggles the mind."

"Very funny. You have no idea how much work it takes to make a car like that look so cool. No way was I going to drive around in some suburban-housewife minivan." He looked at her, hard. "I'm still the guy I was, and if people can't take that it comes in a wheeled version now, it's their problem."

It was an admirable thought, but his words came with such a defiant edge that Heather wondered how many times a week Max chewed someone's head off for an ill-phrased remark or just plain ignorance about life with a disability. Bitterness did that to some men. "Maybe that's just it. Maybe Simon hasn't figured out who he is yet. I had no idea who I was in high school—I just bumbled around most of the time trying to stay out of the sights of all those mean cheerleader types." She borrowed Max's measurement. "I suppose I'd say I was a lot closer to Simon than thugs like Kikowitz."

"Thugs like me?" Again the disarming smile, the penitent hoodlum with his hand over his heart.

"I don't know too many thugs who would round

up a bunch of wheelchairs to play basketball with a geeky kid and two hapless ladies." She was going to say *girls,* but hadn't she chided Max for the label earlier?

"Don't call my sister *hapless*. She was in the army, you know." He wheeled a careless arc around the front walkway, ending up a foot or two closer to her than his earlier position. "So let me guess— 4-H Club? Junior Librarians of America? Church choir?" He did not list them with any admiration— that was certain.

"Art, mostly. I kept to myself a lot. And not choir, but church youth group."

"I knew it." Max executed a spin while he rolled his head back. "One of *those.*"

"Hey, cut that out. I had a…good time in high school." That was at least partially true. Some of high school had been great, but she'd learned her sophomore year what Simon already knew: high school wasn't kind to sick or injured kids.

Max stopped his maneuvers. "No, you didn't."

Heather froze.

"Girls who had awesome times in high school do not come back as guidance counselors. You want to help people. And you want to help people because you don't want anyone to go through what you did."

"Where do you get off making assumptions like that?"

Max threw his hands in the air. "Hey, don't get

all up about it. Do you know how many physical therapists I've had since my accident? How many counselors and docs? Pretty soon it gets easy to recognize the type, that's all."

"Oh, yes, JJ told me you used to tear through a therapist a week back at the beginning. A paragon of empathy." That wasn't particularly fair to throw back at him, but for Heather, his attitude struck an old nerve. "Look—" she forced herself to soften her voice when Max's eyes grew hard and dark "—I want you to help Simon, and I think you might actually be able to. But not if you dump him into some labeled box based on your own experience. Simon's had his disability his entire life—he's never known anything different. You need to respect who he is, not who you want him to be, or this will never work."

Max didn't reply at first. He looked down, fiddling with a joint on his chair. "Okay, I get it." When he raised his eyes again, the edge in his features was replaced by something else. Determination? She couldn't quite tell. "What do you want to happen from all this?"

"What do you mean?"

"I don't know if you want Simon to be happy, to be less of a target or to be able to punch Kikowitz out. What's the end goal here?"

She thought carefully before she answered. "I want Simon not to be afraid of who he is or what

Kikowitz might do to him. He's brilliant, you know. Simon's one of the smartest kids at our school. I want him to enjoy coming here, not dread it."

Max didn't appear to have an immediate answer to that. After what she hoped was a thoughtful pause, he said, "You want him to be able to take risks?"

"He needs a few outlets, I'll admit that."

Max pivoted to face her. "Then we go sailing. You, me and Simon on Saturday afternoon. That way we both can convince the geek there's more to life than Math Club."

"Don't call him a geek. And how did you know Simon was in Math Club?"

"*Puh-lease.* I saw two calculators in his backpack. The dock behind Jones River Sports, two o'clock. You're in charge of permission slips and snacks."

Heather tucked her hands into her pockets. "Who said you could take over here?"

"Eleven therapists," he called as he started down the ramp, clicking the remote starter on his car to send it roaring to life as he descended. "Actually twelve, if you count the one who lasted ten minutes. And four nurses. And there was an intern at Adventure Access who—"

"Okay!" Heather shouted as Max somehow made the engine rev before he even got into the car. "I get the picture."

Chapter Three

Max checked his watch again Saturday afternoon. Since when did he get nervous about stuff like this? Chronically late, he didn't have a leg to stand on—if he could stand—about anyone's punctuality. Still, Simon's dad seemed like the guy to show up ten minutes early, not twenty minutes late. And where was Heather? He wheeled the length of the dock again, needlessly checking the ropes that tied the *Sea Legs* to the dock, frustrated with how much he'd managed to invest in one kid's sailing lesson.

It was the look in Simon's eyes that did him in. That heartbreaking eagerness at the mention of going sailing nearly instantly squashed by a dad's harping voice. Parents were hard enough to take at that age as it was. To have all that other stuff loaded on top, then compounded by kids like Kikowitz?

Kids like he'd been?

The faces of all the kids he'd ever bullied had

haunted him last night. He saw Simon's face every time he shut his eyes, and it was making him crazy. Sleepless, fidgety and just plain nuts.

The sound of tires on gravel hit his ears, and he looked up, expecting the Williamses' big red van. Instead, a small tan sedan pulled into the parking area and Heather climbed out of the nondescript little car. Shoulders slumped, head slightly down, Heather's body broadcast what he'd begun to suspect: Simon wasn't showing.

His understanding—and annoyance—must have been clear on his face, for all Heather said when she walked onto to the dock was "I'm sorry."

Max grunted. It was a better choice than the nasty language currently running in his head.

"I've been on the phone with Brian Williams, trying to convince him Simon would be safe, but—"

"But hooligans like Max Jones can't be trusted with his precious son—oh, I can just hear the speech."

She set down the loudly patterned tote bag she was carrying and eased onto the dock's little bench. "It's not about you."

"Oh, not all about me, but I can just imagine what Simon's dad thinks of someone like me." He flipped open the equipment locker's lid and tossed the third life jacket back inside.

He was picking up the second one when she put

out a hand to stop him. "So I guess we're not going, huh?" Disappointment tinged her words.

Max looked up, life jacket still in his hand, surprised. "No, we can still go." He'd just assumed she'd ditch the day with Simon not coming. Sail alone, just with her? He'd have to go so *slow* and be so *nice*.

"I sort of want to know how this whole rigging works." She gestured toward the specially modified sailboat, covering her tracks with a "professional curiosity" that didn't quite pass muster. She frowned and crossed her arms when she reached the back of the boat. "*Sea Legs?* Really?"

"I thought that was particularly clever, actually. Much better than my first choice."

Her brows knotted together. "I'm almost afraid to ask."

"The *Crip Ship.* JJ thought that a bit confrontational."

Heather laughed. "Max Jones? Confrontational? Imagine my surprise."

Max spread his arms. "Got me where I am today." He tossed her the life jacket. "Hop in. I'll hand over your bag and cast us off." Wheeling over to the bag, he picked it up. It weighed a ton. "There had better be decent snacks in here."

"Homemade brownies, watermelon and some of the firehouse root beer."

Max handed over the bag as he rolled on board

after her. "Someone ought to call Simon and tell him what he's missing." He pulled the ramp up and stowed it in its special spot alongside the keel.

"I think he knows." Heather's voice sounded like he felt. Disappointed and not a little miffed. "This would have been so good for him."

Max liked the way that sounded. Ever since he'd wheeled into Heather's office, he'd gotten the vibe from her that he was a poor substitute for whatever mentor she'd had in mind. It bugged him that Heather hadn't judged him capable of helping someone. Then again, no one was more surprised than him that he'd even cared to take the whole thing on.

He pointed to the bowline. "Undo that knot and pull the line aboard, will you?"

While she climbed up to the front of the boat, Max transferred himself from his chair and into the swiveling seat on rails that allowed him to move freely about the boat. It wasn't a particularly graceful maneuver, and he preferred having her attention diverted elsewhere. Once settled, he collapsed his wheelchair and stowed it in a compartment. Pulling the jib tight, Max felt the singular, blissful sensation of the boat under way. Even before his injury, nothing felt like pulling out onto the river. Now that gravity was often his enemy, the river gave him even more freedom to unwind his nerves. *Sea Legs* may be a mildly tacky joke to some, but it was actually close to how he saw the boat. Anything that gave Max speed and movement gave him life. They counterbalanced all the parts of his life that had become slow and cumbersome since falling from that cliff a little over a year ago.

In a matter of minutes, *Sea Legs* was under way, slicing her way through the Gordon River and catching the perfect breeze that blew through the warm September afternoon. Heading upriver and upwind, he angled the boat toward the opposite shore, ready to "tack" back and forth as the craft moved against the current and into the wind. He watched Heather settle into one of the seats closer to the bow, the breeze tumbling through her hair.

"You're different here than at school," he offered, liking how she angled her face up toward the sunshine. "Not so serious."

She shot him a look. "I take my job seriously. Don't you?"

Max shrugged and tightened up a line. "I don't have a serious job. I'm…enthusiastic about it, but Adventure Access is about making fun, so it's not the kind of job you ought to take seriously."

Heather brought her knees up and hugged them. He found himself staring at her bright pink toenails peeking out of the blue thong sandals she wore. Funny the details that don't come out at the office. Max spent a lot of time noticing feet—now that his weren't much use—and she had ridiculously cute toes that wiggled when she realized he was staring at them.

"Are you serious about anything?" she asked, shifting to tuck her legs underneath her and blushing. Some part of Max was highly entertained that he'd made her blush. What kind of woman wore sensible clear polish on her nails but bright pink on her hidden toes?

"I've been seriously injured. Been listed in 'serious condition' at Lincoln General." He tied off the line. "And I've been in serious trouble lots of times."

She looked more disappointed than annoyed. "What does it take to get a straight answer out of you?"

That was a loaded question. His boss and now brother-in-law, Alex Cushman, had asked pretty much the same thing before bringing him on board at Adventure Access. Nobody seemed willing to take a smart aleck at his word these days—they all wanted to see some deep and serious version of him, as if what he'd been through didn't supply enough credentials. "It takes a straight question. Duck, by the way—we're coming about and the boom is going to come across the boat."

"Okay," she said as she ducked. "Straight question. What did it feel like?"

It was obvious what she meant by "it." "When you cut to the chase, you really cut to the chase, huh?" He had a couple of stock answers to insensitive questions like that—mostly asked by curious kids who didn't know better or adults who only wanted gory, tragic details—but opted against using them. He'd asked her for a straight question, after all. He just hadn't counted on "straight" going to "serious."

"You don't have to tell me. It's none of my business."

"No." Max was surprised to find he didn't feel any of the irritation that kind of question generally raised. He actually wanted to tell her. It must be some kind of empathetic-counselor trick. "It's okay. But it's not especially pretty."

She didn't reply, just leaned one elbow on the bow behind her and looked ready to listen. So he told her.

"I wanted to die."

Heather swallowed hard. Max said it so matter-of-factly. As if *I wanted to die* was like *my left shoulder hurt.* All her counselor training left her no response to his casual attitude.

He actually laughed—a dark half laugh, but still, it sounded wildly inappropriate to her—and she cringed at the sound. "That's horrible," she said, not exactly sure if she meant his feelings that night or his disturbing attitude now.

"Horrible, tragic, devastating—pick your sad word. I've heard them all. Everybody was being so kind and vague and optimistic, but it didn't fool me.

People get that look in their eyes, you know? The one they cover up in a second but you still catch it?"

She did know, but she didn't say anything.

"I think I knew right when I fell that something really serious had happened, but I don't remember hardly anything from that night. I don't remember the helicopter ride—which is rotten, by the way, because I think that would have been cool—or the hospital or surgery or really anything until about a day later. And even my memories from those first days are sort of blurry." Max pivoted the seat and shifted a bit down the rails, adjusting his position as the boat picked up a bit of speed. Heather felt the wind lift her hair and the sun warm her shoulders. It was easy to see why Max craved time on this boat.

"The first thing I clearly remember," he went on, his voice still remarkably conversational, "is waking up in the middle of the night and trying to get up out of bed—I think I wanted to go find JJ or something. That was the moment when I really, truly figured out that I couldn't feel my legs. Like the world just stopped at my hips." He pretended to busy himself with some adjustment to the rigging, but even without a counseling degree, Heather could've seen he couldn't look her in the eye while talking about the trauma. His eyes darted everywhere around the boat but at her, and she could see how hard his hands gripped the tiller. Why even pretend this was an easy memory? What had made her think it would be a good idea to ask?

Max cleared his throat and shifted. "I remember pinching my thigh, hard, and feeling nothing. Zip. Nada. Then all the tubes and nurses and Mom showing up clicked in my head, and I knew. Alone, in the dark, I just *knew.* And I decided it would be better if I stopped breathing, right there and then. It was like I didn't even have enough life left in me to get mad. I was hollow, empty…just gone, like my legs."

He ventured a glance up at her, and she felt the severity in his eyes as fiercely as if he'd grabbed her hand. "So that's what it was like. *Lousy*'s not really a strong enough word, if you get what I mean."

She had a way-more-than-lousy memory like that. The scars running down her left hip and thigh shouted memories that made her feel hollow and "just gone." Only she couldn't brandish them like Max did. There had been another man in her life, years back, who pushed his pain out onto the world like that. Mike had forced his illness on people, daring them to cope with the nasty details, almost looking down on her when she couldn't do it that way. Heather could count the number of people who had seen her scarred leg on the fingers of one hand. "I'm sorry," she whispered, not knowing how else to respond.

Max shook his head, his sardonic smile mocking her compassion. "You know, everybody says that.

I've got enough I'm-sorrys to fill this river twice over. That always struck me as funny, 'cause it never accomplishes anything."

"Oh, yes, you make it clear no one's allowed to feel sorry for you." That came out a bit sharper than she'd planned, but some part of her was having trouble swallowing Max's nonstop bravado. Sure, he laughed off his huge trauma—and looked down on anyone else who couldn't do the same—but he wasn't fooling anyone. He thought all that casual charm hid his dark edge, but it didn't. Not to her.

"I don't think Simon wants people feeling sorry for him, either. I think half his problem comes from how much people coddle him." Max waved his hand around the boat. "See anything life threatening here? Any deep, dark dangers?"

"Only one, and he's just as dangerous on land."

Max jutted a finger at her. "See? That's *exactly* what I'm talking about. Would you make a crack like that at Simon? Would you give him the respect of thinking him strong enough to take it?"

"Simon is a fifteen-year-old boy who's sick."

"No," Max nearly shouted, jerking a line in tighter so the boat picked up speed. "He's *not* sick. That's just it, Heather—he's not sick any more than I am. Okay, his legs don't work right. My legs don't work at all, but I can do almost anything I want, while he…" Max growled and slid the seat so fast down the rails that Heather felt the whole boat shake when the chair locked into a new position. "Simon and I have been texting each other since the basketball game. His mom cuts up his meat, for crying out loud. The only thing limiting him is his parents. If he's having social problems, it's their fault."

"That's not fair! My mom had to help me like that after I got hurt, and—" Heather snapped her mouth shut, beyond angry with herself for letting that slip. She angled away from Max, pretending—uselessly—to look out over the water while he took the boat into another turn. She couldn't go anywhere; she was trapped on this boat with Max Jones and an admission she'd give anything to take back right now. The silence on board was so thick she felt paralyzed herself.

He stayed quiet the whole way across the river, which surprised her. She'd expected Max to pry the rest of the story out of her, but he didn't. She felt him looking at her, sensed his gaze even though she kept her eyes on the river.

Finally, as he turned the boat around again, Heather dared to look his way. His whole face had changed. His face showed warmth and understanding, not the defiance that seemed to be his constant expression. "What happened?" An hour ago, she wouldn't have believed Max capable of such a tender tone.

She didn't like the idea of his knowing the details. Those were private. But Max Jones needed to know he was not the only person on earth to suffer a life-changing accident. And out here on the water, Heather felt as if the secret could be safely contained. "I was burned. In an accident. My junior year of high school." Even those vague details made her feel wildly exposed, and she hugged her knees again, clutching the scarred thigh close and away from the world. "And whether or not you think it's *useless,* I'm still very, very sorry it happened."

She expected him to press her for details, but Max seemed to sense she'd taken a huge step in admitting just the basic facts. He didn't pry or challenge her need for privacy; he just let her be quiet amid the wind and water. When they pulled the boat up to the dock a peaceful hour later, Heather conceded that there might be more to Max Jones than she'd realized.

Chapter Four

Jeannie Owens adjusted the gift basket's ribbon Monday afternoon with an artist's touch before pushing it across the counter to Heather. "That ought to do the parents' night fund-raising auction proud, don't you think?"

"Sure."

The Sweet Treats candy-shop owner furrowed her brow. "I was hoping for a more enthusiastic reaction. My chocolate-covered caramels are supposed to be sought after, not barely tolerated."

Heather knew very well how "sought after" Jeannie's caramels were. Too well, if her bathroom scale was any indication. "Sorry. This is fabulous—it's even bigger than last year's."

"But…" Jeannie cued, raising one eyebrow in concern rather than judgment.

Heather sighed. "It's not you or the candy. I'm just preoccupied, I guess."

"Trouble at school?" Heather knew Jeannie's son had encountered his share of problems freshman year at GFHS. While the school had tried to offer guidance, the real solution had come from Fire Marshal Chad Owens, who'd not only befriended Jeannie's son, Nick, but fallen for Jeannie herself. Nick was now an exemplary senior and one of Heather's favorite happy endings for this graduating class.

"I'm worried about Simon Williams. Actually, I'm worried about what Jason Kikowitz might do to Simon Williams." She usually made it a point not to give names when talking about school issues, but Jeannie had particular insight regarding a bully's influence on a boy facing problems.

Heather watched Jeannie try to place Simon's name. It was no effort to place Jason's—everyone who had a student at GFHS knew who "that Kikowitz boy" was. "Williams...Brian Williams's boy? Chad said Brian was all huffed about something that happened at school. Now it makes sense." Her eyes filled with compassion. "As if high school isn't hard enough. To have to do it in a wheelchair must feel impossible."

"Simon'll make it. He's such a good kid. Unsure of himself, but so smart."

"But a target for guys like Kikowitz, I'm sure." Jeannie pulled the top off a large glass jar on her counter that was filled with her signature chocolate-covered caramels and tilted the opening toward

Heather. "You've got your hands full. That deserves one on the house."

Heather couldn't help but pull a caramel from the jar, sure she would regret it later. Even if Jeannie campaigned that the world's problems could be solved with enough sugar and chocolate, Heather's hips put up valid resistance to the idea. "He's got so much potential. I care a lot about this one. Too much, maybe."

"No such thing," Jeannie said, sliding the canister back into place. "Don't you ever stop caring too much—it's what makes you so good at what you do." Jeannie had a vibrancy about her that Heather loved. And she had a great family despite knowing a lot of trials in her life. Sure, Heather came into Sweet Treats for the chocolate, but she came in just as much for the friendship and support. "I wondered about him when the family moved in over the summer," Jeannie went on. "Chad says Brian is a terrific father. Really engaged and involved."

"He's devoted to Simon—no doubt about it. Only I think this year is going to be a challenge."

"Jason Kikowitz is good at that." Jeannie polished off the last of her caramel and licked the lingering chocolate off her fingers.

"More than that, actually."

"What do you mean?"

"Well, you remember how hard it is to loosen up on the reins when your child enters high school."

That was a nicer way of putting it than Max's *he needs to back off.* "I think Mr. and Mrs. Williams are going to have a tough time granting Simon the independence to make his own mistakes, especially with the fine start Kikowitz has supplied." It was hard for most parents to strike that balance—Heather's voice mail and email filled every September with parents trying too hard to manage their kids' high school experiences—but doubly so in Simon's case.

Jeannie's face softened. "It's the hardest thing in the world. Which is why the world needs you. Have you decided how you're going to help Simon?"

"Actually, JJ came up with the idea to have Max mentor him."

Jeannie raised both her eyebrows. "Chad mentioned JJ told him something about a basketball game?" Her expression appeared hopeful. "That sounds fun." Yes, well, Jeannie had always been famous for her unflinching optimism.

"It was…sort of. He and Simon certainly seemed to connect, but let's just say I have doubts Max will be much of a calming influence."

"Calm?" Jeannie laughed. "Max Jones hasn't been calm a day in his life. Did you see his car? Nick was drooling over the flame paint job the other day."

The car. Everyone in Gordon Falls knew that car and had an opinion of both its look-at-me paint and its here-I-come roar. "Yep. Can't miss it—that's for sure."

Jeannie leaned on the counter with both elbows. "Well, I understand why you're worried, but you never know. Max might surprise you."

"He's already been a surprise—and not necessarily the good kind." She hadn't expected Simon to take to Max so strongly, nor had she expected Max to take a shine to Simon with the strength that he had. Of course, she'd wanted to put a halt to the thing at first, but there was something about the combination of Max and Simon that wouldn't let her give up on the pair just yet. Maybe it had something to do with the way Simon had laughed in triumph at the end of their basketball game. She got the sense he didn't laugh like that very often.

Jeannie came out from behind the counter to sit on one of the sunny yellow window-seat cushions that lined one side of her shop. "I can't help thinking it takes someone like Max to stand up to someone like Kikowitz."

"That's just it," Heather agreed.

"Then again," Jeannie went on, "if I had to pick someone just as likely to make everything worse, it might be Max."

"And *that's* just it." Heather sat down beside Jeannie. "Sure, Simon thinks he's terrific right now. He looks cool. He talks up a great game. But I don't really know him—he seems all swagger and no substance. Max could have too much influence—and all the wrong kind—on a kid like that."

"Alex puts a lot of faith in him, and I don't think Alex would do that if he didn't see something in Max that was more than just a snazzy paint job. He's willing to help, right? Can't be all that bad if he's at least willing to lend a hand."

The memory of Max's thundering muffler as it roared out of the school parking lot gave Heather enough reason to doubt Jeannie's optimism. "I'm not so sure. Max is very…sure of himself. Actually, he's arrogant, confrontational and rather tactless."

Jeannie wound one piece of hair around a finger, thinking. "Maybe Max is exactly the kind of guy Simon needs. What boy wouldn't want to know you can be in a wheelchair and still be that cool? I know he's a bit over-the-top, but Nick thinks he's 'sick'—and evidently that's a compliment." Jeannie laughed. "He's not exactly hard to look at, and all those adventures he goes on…"

"He's a walking…*rolling* barrel of 'look at me.' He's so busy shoving his circumstances in your face that he forgets you're even in the room." Max wasn't the first man in her life to be so busy being a cause that he'd forgotten how to be a person. She wasn't eager to repeat the experience.

Jeannie pushed off the wall and headed toward

the cash register as a knot of giggling girls pushed into the store. "Well, I'll give him one thing."

Heather settled her handbag higher on her shoulder and picked up the massive gift basket. "What?"

"He knows how to get a rise out of you."

Tuesday afternoon, Max rolled into Heather's office in response to a phone-message summons.

"It's one-thirty." She scowled at the big white standard-issue school clock on her wall when he arrived. "I asked you to come by in the morning. It was kind of urgent."

"I had an appointment. I got here as soon as I could afterward." Normally he didn't mention the dozens of monthly medical visits his condition required, but he wanted her to know life wasn't all fun and games for him, even if he was in the fun-and-games business. "My neurologist is a nice guy but not nice enough to ditch just because you need backup."

She didn't seem capable of pulling off a mean face. "Who says I need backup?"

"It doesn't take a rocket scientist to know your voice mail is probably chock-full of worried calls from Brian Williams today. Come on—I saw that one coming a mile off. Has he asked you to keep me away from his precious impressionable son yet?"

He'd nailed it; he could see it in her eyes. "Do

you have to ride the man so hard? He cares about his son."

He wheeled farther into her office. She'd moved her guest chair to the side to accommodate his chair. That settled somewhere soft in the back of his brain. "It's been my experience that there's a very thin line between care and smother. Especially when you're fifteen. Did you see Simon's eyes when his father pulled up after the basketball game? Did you hear how even the school ramp made Pops nervous?"

Heather leaned one elbow on her desk. "How long, exactly, has it been since you were fifteen?"

He didn't want to give her the satisfaction of a number. "A while."

"Well, then, think back a while and remember that every student his age—disability or not—is mortified by everything their parents do. It's practically rule number one in the high schooler's handbook."

"Hey, you just made a joke." He angled himself around to dig a hand into the bag he kept attached to the back of his chair.

She narrowed her eyes at him. "Really?" Heather was just so much fun to tick off, Max suspected he was going to get in trouble here far faster than his usual rate—which was pretty fast as it was.

"Well—" he found what he was looking for and pulled it out of the bag "—it just makes it easier to give you this." Scooting up to her desk, he planted a bright pink rubber duck made to look like a flamingo on top of her files. It made a ridiculous squeaking sound as he did so, its little black rubber sunglasses squishing in on its hooked flamingo beak before inflating back into shape. Normally he wasn't the gift type—barely remembering birthdays and such—but this had caught his eye in the hospital gift shop. The tone of her voice mail had made it clear Brian Williams had clouded up and rained all over her morning, and he'd wanted to cheer her up. "It's a flamingo rubber duck, which is kind of a joke when you think about it." When she looked genuinely startled, he added, "For your collection. And for not getting here until now."

She reached for it, and he could see she was holding back a smile. "You know, a phone call to let me know your time frame would have been all I needed." Her words were all *you shouldn't have* but her eyes were *I love it*. How did someone so transparent make any headway with predators like teenagers?

She placed the flamingo-duck right next to the one he'd toyed with at their first meeting. "Yes, Mr. Williams expressed his concern."

"Is that teacher-speak for *he chewed my ear off?*"

"Let's just say I think it will take more than rubber waterfowl to bring Mr. Williams around. He was curious…suspicious, actually, that you clearly did not include him in your sailing invitation. That, more than any physical danger, is what kept Simon off your boat Saturday."

Max didn't like where this was heading. "He's jealous?"

"Could you be serious for one minute here? Schools have to tread carefully where and how we let adults alone with students. And there are really good reasons—really awful ones, actually—why those rules are in place. He's in the right here, Max. I should have never okayed that boat outing."

Max had no patience for this kind of red-tape stupidity. "You've gotta be kidding me. You were going along. Brian Williams knows who I am. He works with my sister. I'm not some creep off the train from the big bad city."

Heather sat back in her chair. "Do you want to help Simon or not?"

"Yes!" He didn't even have to think about the answer. Simon's eyes had been haunting him all weekend. He was like a walking poster child for everything Adventure Access was about—giving people with disabilities the chance to be regular people and have the kinds of fun that everyone craved. Max didn't just want to help Simon; some part of him *needed* to help the little guy.

That clearly wasn't the answer she was expecting. Wow, did she really think he'd walk away just because Daddy got hot under the collar? That bugged him more than Williams's unfounded suspicions.

"Then we've got to work within the boundaries here. Simon's dad sees him as vulnerable, and he's not all wrong. This is hard for any parent, much less one with as much to worry about as Brian Williams has on his plate."

She was right, of course. Some part of him recognized that. He'd gone in full blast, letting Williams's perfectly natural responses get under his skin because of how much *he* hated being coddled. And while she was eons better now, hadn't his own mother been ten times worse than Brian Williams when he was first injured? "Yeah." He owed her at least that much of an acknowledgment.

"If it helps, I think he really should go out on your boat. It's a beautiful boat, and it's fascinating to watch how it works and you work on it. It's just not the right starting point. Basketball? Now, that was a good first step for a lot of reasons. Can we think of something else like that? Something that can take place here on school property?"

"Williams is going to supervise, isn't he?"

"Yes." Her eyes flicked down at the admission. "He's asked to be present." She looked up. "Think you can play nice here?"

Normally, Max's reply to a request like that would have been a resounding *Not on your life!* Only it was as if Simon's pleading eyes watched him even though the kid wasn't even in the room. "How are you at Ping-Pong?"

That smile could have made him buy twelve flamingo-ducks in rainbow colors. "I happen to be pretty good. Thursday afternoon?"

He could move his marketing-team meeting. It'd mean he would have to get up an hour earlier than normal—something he only did in the most dire circumstances—but he'd do it. "Let me make a few calls."

Chapter Five

"Got 'em!"

Heather watched in amazement Thursday afternoon as Simon edged his chair in front of his father to nail the match's winning shot. In the last half of the game, Simon had seemed to come alive right before her eyes, showing a determination and enthusiasm she'd not ever seen from him. It was the first time she could use the phrase *young man* to describe Simon. Lots of boys made the transition from "boy" to "young man" in their first year of high school, but she'd never seen the transformation happen quite so dramatically.

Max had noticed the change, as well; she could tell by the way he caught her eye in between volleys or when Simon made a particularly spectacular shot. Simon wasn't the only one making surprising changes right in front of her. Max had gone out of his way to "play nice" with Brian Williams. Right down to the nondescript polo shirt instead of his usual T-shirt bearing a wild message. She'd spent the first game trying not to notice what the light blue color did for Max's eyes. JJ had told her Max had rolled up in a tux for her wedding, and suddenly she wanted to see the pictures of what that looked like. Max Jones, for all his edgy attire, cleaned up *very* nice.

"Hey, Dad, watch this!"

Heather gasped as Simon made an attempt to pop one of the wild wheelies Max was known for—and succeeded only in toppling himself out of the chair. Mr. Williams let out a "Don't do that!" and flew out of his own chair—for everyone had to play in chairs again to even the odds—grabbing Simon's arm before Heather even had a chance to blink.

"I'm fine!" Simon declared, pulling his arm out of his father's grasp. The air in the gym suddenly thickened. Heather didn't know quite what to do.

Max did. In a matter of seconds, Max spun over next to Simon and proceeded to catapult himself out of his own chair. Now there were two people on the ground, with Heather and Mr. Williams standing in shock beside them.

"Didn't that hurt?" Simon asked, as stunned as anyone else in the room.

"Not if I can't feel anything below my waist. Of course, I wouldn't advise this as a general practice, but it's easier to show you how to get up than to sit there and explain it."

"I can help him get up," Mr. Williams interjected, reaching between Max and Simon.

"No, Dad," Simon protested. "Let me see how Max does this."

Mr. Williams looked ready to object, but Heather walked over and gently touched his elbow. "Let him try," she whispered, seeing the panic in the father's eyes. "You can step in if he gets in trouble."

"What do I do?" Simon was as cool as a cucumber and obviously not a bit hurt.

"First—" Max winked "—you find somewhere else for the people around you to look because this isn't pretty. Point out a flower or a puppy or something."

Simon managed a wry grin. "They're staring right at us."

"Well." Max elbowed Simon as if being sprawled out on the gym floor were all part of the plan. "Think of something."

Simon pointed clear across the gym. "Hey, Dad, could you go get the Ping-Pong ball where it landed over in the corner?"

Mr. Williams did not look as if he cared for this one bit. Heather offered him an encouraging smile, eyebrows raised in a silent invitation to just play along.

The pause before Mr. Williams said, "Sure,

son," felt excruciating. He pinched the bridge of his nose as he stepped away from Max and Simon and walked across the gym floor.

As she followed Mr. Williams, swallowing the urge to turn and look at whatever it was Max was teaching Simon, she heard the smile in Max's voice as he instructed, "Okay, pull your chair over here and put your left hand up on this."

She walked in the direction Simon had pointed, catching Mr. Williams's eye one more time. "I know that was hard," she said, keenly aware that she truly had no idea how hard it might have been.

Brian Williams was trying; she had to give him that. He wanted to turn and watch as badly as Heather did—it was all over his face—but he made a show of searching for the little white ball both of them quickly realized wasn't anywhere near where Simon had sent them.

After he heard Max's overloud, "There you go, back upright," Heather turned and threw up her hands in mock failure, inwardly delighted at the beaming and seated Simon—right next to a seated and slightly winded Max. Something hummed under her ribs as she realized what it had cost Max to toss himself out of his chair like that.

"Hey, look, Dad—the ball was right here all the time."

Did Simon actually just wink?

"No kidding," Mr. Williams said, his voice a mixture of emotions Heather couldn't quite read. Was he proud of his son? Or annoyed at being "played"?

"Yeah. And I'm fine," Simon repeated.

"Upright and awesome." Max held up a fist and Simon bumped it in the universal high school sign of victory and admiration. "Only, I'd hold back on the wheelies till you get better at them. Knocks the cool right out of the whole thing if you tumble like we just did."

"True." Simon looked at Max. "We still beat you."

Max pasted a dejected look on his face. "You and your dad creamed me and Ms. Browning. I'm not used to losing—we'd better find something else to play next time where I can be sure I'll win."

"Then it can't be chess," Mr. Williams offered. "He beats me every time."

Surely this would bring some crack about chess's geek factor. Max probably stuffed the Chess Club into lockers on a weekly basis in high school. Heather saw the barb come across his face, then watched as he swallowed whatever wisecrack was on the tip of his tongue. "Not really my thing, chess. But I'll think of something and run it by Ms. Browning and your dad before I set it up, okay?"

Heather had to work to keep her mouth from dropping open. Somehow she was sure Max Jones never sought approval for anything—he definitely seemed more like the "do what you want and apologize later if you get caught" type. Was Max doing a little maturing of his own?

After they'd packed up the equipment and walked Simon and his dad to their car—and Max had gotten a lot of mileage out of a "walk you to your car" bit—Heather found herself at a loss for how to deal with this new side of Max.

She knew where to start, at least. Sitting down on the short wall that framed the school steps, she folded her hands in her lap. "Thank you."

"For what?" His face told her he knew exactly for what.

"I want to say for behaving, but that doesn't sound very good." She fiddled with her watch, suddenly finding his eyes a little too intense. "You know what you did back there. I just want you to know I appreciate it."

"You mean launching myself onto the floor so Simon wouldn't feel like a train wreck? That was kind of fun, actually. Although, I expect I'll find a few bruises in the morning."

"Did it hurt?" The minute the words left her mouth, they felt like the most insensitive thing she could have picked to ask.

Max held her gaze for a moment—something that made her insides buzz. The man had astounding, expressive eyes. "It's okay to ask stuff like that, you know. I don't mind. If I think you're stepping over the line, believe me, I'll tell you." He shifted in his chair. "No, it didn't hurt. Nothing hurts. I'm deadweight from the waist down. But it also means I can't tell if I've hurt myself, so flinging myself out of chairs isn't the smartest thing I could be doing. That was more of an impulse."

"It was a good one—I mean, provided you didn't get hurt. Did you see Simon's eyes?"

"Couldn't miss it. Kid lit up like a firecracker. Do you think that's the first time he's told his dad to back off a bit?" Max was as excited about Simon's confidence level as she was.

"Could be. And you found an appropriate way to make that happen."

He got that heart-slayer gleam in his eyes again. "Look at me, Mr. Appropriate. Who knew I had it in me?"

She hadn't. Up until today, Heather had worried that he would grow bored and skip out on Simon in a matter of days. Looking at him now, she could see his investment in Simon was surprising even him. "You did a great thing today. I hope you know that." Before she could think better of it, she nodded toward his shirt. "You even dressed for the occasion."

"You noticed." He preened the collar on his polo shirt, grinning. "Had to dig deep in the closet for this. Not a lot of call for business-casual attire at Adventure Access."

"Not a suit-and-tie kind of office?"

"Are you kidding? This counts for formal wear at AA."

The visage of a tuxedoed Max at the wedding where Alex married Max's sister popped back up in her imagination. *He must have had ladies lined up at his feet when he could walk.*

The horrid nature of that thought shot through her—what an awful, terrible thing to think! Why was Max Jones such a mental minefield for her good sense?

"Okay, what was that?"

She hated that he noticed. "Nothing."

He pointed at her. "You just had a cripple thought."

"A *what?*"

"Aw, come on—you think I can't tell? Someone has a thought, usually to do with my paralysis, that they think is totally awful and cruel, usually because it is, and their face goes all screwy like yours just did. I call them 'cripple thoughts,' because that's the most offensive word for what I am."

She felt horrendously exposed. Guilty and trapped. What on earth was she supposed to do? Why did Max feel as if he had to shove the awkwardness in everyone's face like this?

"Look, just get over it, okay? It's easier if you admit this is weird. I hate tiptoeing around the issue. You had a cripple thought. It's gonna happen. I'm used to it. I can see it a mile off."

Heather launched up off the wall. "Why do you

do that? It was a terrible thing to think and I'm already ashamed of myself, so why are you making me feel so bad about it when you were just so incredibly nice to Simon?"

Max spun around to follow her. "There. See? You can yell at me for being a jerk just like any other guy. Glad we got that out of the way."

She turned to look at him. "You're awful—you know that?" But, she had to admit, the tension had just evaporated. Crude as it was, he was breaking down her misconceptions about him one at a time. Ten minutes ago she would not have felt free to tell him he was awful. He'd sensed her pity even before she had, and he'd called her on it because he didn't want pity from her. Or anyone.

"*Awful* is a personal specialty. Just don't sugarcoat things for me on account of my wheels, okay? I can take just about anything but that." He motioned to the wall again, silently asking her to sit down so they could be eye to eye again. Heather was coming to realize how important that courtesy was to him.

"So," he said, rubbing his hands together, "how about we start that part over?"

Heather cleared her throat. She would do as he asked; she would treat him as she would treat any other person who had just done something incredibly nice for Simon. "Can I buy you a cup of coffee and a slice of pie at Karl's to show my appreciation?"

It was fun to be the one surprising him for once.

He wasn't expecting that. "Celebrate our little victory over helicopter dad?"

Heather rolled her eyes. "When you put it that way…"

"No. I mean, I won't put it that way. Which means yes. Yes to coffee. If you're buying."

"I am."

"Only if I drive."

How had she known there'd be a catch to his yes? "You drive?"

"Yep. If you're willing to ride in the flaming toaster, I'll know you really mean it."

"Is *everything* a test with you?"

There was that glint again. "Only the good stuff."

She might regret this. "I'll go get my handbag—since I'm paying and all." She walked toward the door, then turned around again. "The *flaming toaster?*"

"JJ's name. Fits."

She didn't know what to say. *I feel that a lot around you,* she thought as she pulled the door open and went inside.

Max punched JJ's number into his cell phone the minute the school door shut behind Heather.

"Hi there," she answered. "I just put the steaks into the marinade."

"I might not make dinner. I don't have a ton of

time to talk, but I'm heading out for coffee with Heather Browning."

Silence greeted his news.

"Look, we can have dinner tomorrow night, right?"

Another long pause. "Max, don't."

Oh, she was a master of the big-sister tone of conviction. "What?"

"You promised me you wouldn't get personal with Heather. She's a friend. You were helping her out. Now you're going to go all Max on her, aren't you?" Max could practically hear her stabbing the steaks with a sharp fork over the phone.

"I'm not doing anything. She invited me out for coffee. A friendly celebration over something good that happened with Simon."

"You don't know how to do friendly, Max. Please don't get into this with Heather."

Now she was getting annoying. "Get into what, exactly?" Sure, Max had left a long line of broken hearts in his wake before his accident, but he hadn't exactly boasted a stuffed social calendar since. "So now that I'm in a wheelchair, the entire female gender is off-limits?"

"You can date anyone you like, Max, as long as it's not Heather."

"Who said I was even dating Heather? Or planning to date her? Jumping to a few conclusions, aren't you?" Max kept one eye on the door. "You're out of line here, JJ."

There was a pause on her end of the line. "I just don't want you…well…you know."

"Wow. Your confidence in me staggers the mind. It's pie and coffee at Karl's, for crying out loud. And she asked. Give me a little credit here."

"Credit or not, you're still blowing Alex and me off for dinner. We've been planning this for two weeks."

She was right about that much. Between her shifts at the firehouse and Alex's schedule, getting together was proving nearly impossible lately. "What if I came by at seven—would that work?"

"Yes. I'd like that." After a moment she added, "I miss you, Max. I used to see you all the time and now—"

"Hey. We're still Max and JJ. Besides, you've got that spiffy new groom to keep you occupied."

"That spiffy new groom also happens to be your boss. Have you considered you were just trying to ditch your boss, too?"

"I'm trying to help a kid out, JJ. That's all this is."

"Look, I just want you to steer clear of Heather in the date department. You know your track record. She's a friend. This could get all kinds of weird, you know?"

It bugged Max that his own sister thought of him as toxic in the boyfriend department. Sure, he wasn't a master of solid relationships, and all her cautiousness hinted at a seriously painful past, but that didn't mean he couldn't be a decent human being over a slice of pie. "It's just coffee, JJ. I gotta go."

"Be nice, Max. Nice? Do you remember how?"

Chapter Six

Max hit the remote-control button that slowly opened the double doors on his adapted Honda Element. Heather was surprised to see the pair of doors open from the middle like French doors, but it made sense given the large opening they formed.

"Ta-da!" Max imitated a trumpet fanfare as if the gates to his castle were being raised. He was always cracking jokes. Max was like a kid that way—ramping up the wisecracks when he was nervous or uncomfortable. The mechanized ramp unfolded, making the drawbridge metaphor a little more apt, and Max waved her on board with a grandiose gesture. "Ladies first. You get to ride like I'm your chauffeur this time. I can put in the passenger seat with a little more notice, but right now my chair goes there. Although I'll warn you, it's not the cleanest car in the world. Just shove everything over on the backseat and make room for yourself."

She walked up the ramp, surprised to see the backseats were a little higher than the front seats. It made her feel like a spectator instead of a passenger; an odd sensation. True to Max's warning, Heather had to move three T-shirts, a fast-food bag and a pair of sports magazines over to make a spot to sit. Max rolled on board and went through the process of securing his chair where the passenger seat usually went, then shifted himself into the driver's seat and rotated it into position.

"It's amazing," Heather said, watching the adaptations. It was both interesting and a little unnerving to be in his car. She couldn't remember the last time she'd even been in the backseat of a car, much less one as tricked out as this.

Max caught her eye in the rearview mirror. "You didn't think I'd drive a minivan, did you?"

"No, the paint job pretty much gives your taste in cars away." He turned the ignition, sending a deafening blast of loud music through the car.

"Sorry!" he hollered as he quickly lowered the volume. "I like it loud." The engine roared to life, loud enough without the music. He really was like a teenage boy in too many ways.

He grinned and adopted a terrible highbrow accent. "To Karl's, madam?"

"Yes, please." She watched in fascination as he worked the hand controls that pulled the car out and into gear. "Was it hard to learn to drive?"

"The hand controls?" Max called over his shoulder. "Not really. I just think of it like a real-live video game. I took out a mailbox my first week, but it's been smooth sailing since then. I had more accidents with my old walking car than I've had with this one."

It was a matter of minutes before he pulled up into the accessible spot around the corner from Karl's Koffee. "I get all the best spots at the mall," he said, doing a spot-on imitation of a teenage girl as he hit the button to reopen the automated doors. She climbed out, then waited on the sidewalk for him to shift into his chair and come down the ramp.

"This is where it gets a bit tricky. Karl's front has steps, so I get to use the secret entrance."

"That sounds fun," she replied.

His eyes darkened a bit. "You'd think, but not really. You can meet me around front if you'd like."

She didn't know if this was another of those diversionary tactics like he'd coached Simon to use or a true invitation. She decided to see Karl's from his point of view. "I'll go for what's behind door number two."

Max's smile was pleased but cautious. They went around to the back of the establishment, where Max hit a doorbell. After about a minute, Karl, the friendly older man who owned the place, pushed open the door. "Maxwell! Saw that boat out on the river the other day—pretty spiffy. It's good to see ya, son. Gimme a second to clear the decks."

Heather felt a twinge of guilt as Karl went back inside. "I didn't even think about the front steps before I suggested Karl's. I'm sorry."

"Don't be." Max almost looked as though he meant it. Was he really okay with her choice, or was he using this as a lesson in how challenging Gordon Falls could be for him? "I was a regular here back before I got hurt, and I've always liked the place. He just has to move a few things to give me a clear shot to the front. He's always good about it, but…" Max finished the thought with weary eyes rather than words. "I can get in easier at Café Homestead, but I like their pie better here. You gave me an excuse to make the extra effort."

"Me, too. Everyone always goes there for pie, but I think it's better here."

The door reopened. "Okay, all set. Corner table's all waiting."

"You rate the corner table at Karl's?" Heather asked. It was always taken when she came here, and it was a favorite spot with the best view out the window.

"Sort of," Max admitted. "It's the only place I fit, so it's a backhanded benefit. Evidently you get a free coffee if Karl has to move you to make room for me." He said it with a cheerful tone Heather didn't fully believe.

He had good reason. Heather was astounded how much effort it took to get Max through the back of the coffeehouse, around the existing tables and settled in the corner spot. It made her feel terrible at how easily she breezed in whenever she felt like it.

"Don't go all pity party on me." He sent her a dismissive grin, tossing back his tousled hair. "I get seated first on the airplane, and if we ever go to Disney World I can get you on Space Mountain without waiting in line. This is nothing. I'm used to it."

She sat back in her chair. "Why did you ever say yes to here if you knew it would be such a hassle?"

"Because it's where you wanted to go." He peered toward the chalkboard that held Karl's daily offerings. "And like you said, the pie is good here. Besides, I like Karl and I don't get to see him as much. They have blueberry today. Awesome." When she stared at him, he added, "Don't you ever do things that are a hassle just because you want to do them?"

Heather thought of the fifty-minute drive she made to her preferred hairstylist. "I suppose I do."

"So, are we just pie celebrating, or did today's victories rate pie a la mode?"

His eyes could stop a train when he smiled like that. "Oh, definitely with ice cream." Karl had walked up, so when Max nodded in her direction, she said, "Dutch apple pie a la mode and coffee, Karl."

Karl wrote on the little green notepad he always used. "And what about you, Hot Wheels?"

"Blueberry. With ice cream. And coffee."

Karl scribbled, then tucked the notepad into his apron pocket. "Done and done. Coming right up, kids."

Heather laughed. "Kids?"

Max looked after the old man as he limped away. "Karl's hip isn't doing so good. Age. I guess to him we're all kids. He told me once that he has a granddaughter about our age, but I've never met her."

"He didn't try to set you up?" Max was handsome and Karl poked his nose in everyone's business.

Max shot her a look that belonged on a pirate. "Would *you* set me up with your granddaughter?"

She laughed at the way he could make fun of himself so easily. "Well, now that you mention it, I suppose I'd hesitate. You drive a flaming toaster, after all."

He laughed, as well, but Heather caught something in the way Max looked at the man. "How long has your dad been gone? JJ told me he passed away, but I never did ask her much more."

"Years." Max tapped his chair. "It's probably for the best. I don't think Pops would have handled this too well. My dad was hard-core military. A 'walk it off' kind of guy who even had trouble when JJ wouldn't re-up after all she'd been through. This isn't a 'walk it off' kind of thing, if you'll pardon the pun."

Heather decided she would try a different approach. "Why do you make so many jokes about it?"

"Why wouldn't I?"

"Well, it's just that you say it doesn't matter, but you make it matter all the time by making cracks about it. Dark, on-the-edge-of-not-quite-so-funny cracks."

Max put both elbows on the table and pasted an enthralled look on his face. "No, really, counselor, tell me straight-out what you think my issues are."

"Close your mouth, son. She's pretty, but she's already sitting with you" came Karl's voice over Heather's shoulder as he put down the two slices of pie. "Don't try so hard."

"This is school related," Heather felt compelled to point out, waiting for Max to back her up.

"Could have fooled me." Karl nudged Max's shoulder. "Nice going, Hot Wheels."

Heather remembered the one reason she didn't come to Karl's more often—it was ground zero for the local gossip chain. Why hadn't she remembered that if she showed up at Karl's with Max, it would take about seventeen minutes for folks to start making inferences? She pulled a notebook out of her handbag and put it on the table with a pen.

"Oh, that'll throw them off for sure," Max whispered loudly.

"You weren't helping."

"It's Karl."

"No, it's everybody. They're staring."

"I'm in a wheelchair with flames painted on the sides. Of course they're staring." He was baiting her, and worse yet, he was enjoying it. "Look." He leaned in. "They could actually be staring for other reasons, but I'm so used to the stares I'd probably never even realize it. You want to go? I'll take you back to school. But I don't think we're going to die from overexposure here."

She felt cornered. If she didn't go, people might start linking her with Max Jones, and she definitely wasn't ready for that. If she did go, she'd look as if she was ashamed to be seen in public with him— or maybe with anyone in a wheelchair—and that wasn't appropriate...or true, either.

Max cut off the end of his slice with his fork. "Okay, my turn. Why do you weird out when people notice you?"

"I don't."

"You do."

"I don't crave attention the way you do, if that's what you're saying."

Max scooped up the piece of pie and put it into his mouth. "Nope, you can't make this one about me. A fine-looking lady shouldn't work so hard to be invisible." He pointed at Heather with his fork.

"Somebody or something taught you to want to hide like that. You've got issues."

She gave him her best "I am in control of this conversation" look. "You are making a lot of assumptions here, Mr. Jones."

He cocked his head to one side. "Have dinner with me."

Her jaw clenched—he hadn't even framed it as a question. "We're already eating pie."

"I've always thought dessert first was a fine culinary strategy. Let's have dinner."

"No." She gave the word all the finality she could muster. She should have known he'd push too hard at anything he did—why not at her?

"Because of the chair?"

"Stop that. I said no. And not because of the chair, but because we are currently working together on a school matter."

He leaned back. "It's because of the chair."

Heather planted her hands on the table. "It's because of the arrogant, pushy man *in* the chair." She let out a breath and began putting the notebook back into her handbag. "I was just trying to be nice, to celebrate all the good you've done with Simon, but I should have known it'd get like this. I'll walk back to school, thanks."

Max put his hands up. "Okay, okay. I'll take it down a notch."

"Or three."

"Fine, I'll take it down four notches. We did good with Simon. Let's have pie and coffee and talk about Simon and I'll keep my dinner plans with Alex and JJ and pretend this never happened."

She glared at him. "You were going to ditch Alex and JJ for dinner?"

"Well, not really. I was pretty sure you'd say no."

Heather put one hand to her forehead. "You are absolutely impossible. You should come with a warning label."

Just then a preschool girl wobbled up, pointing at the flames on the side of his chair. As Max was raising a hand to wave hello, the mom rushed up, gushed out an embarrassed apology and pulled the child away.

His gaze followed the child, who craned her neck around against her mother's tug to look again at Max. "I already do."

Max wheeled up alongside the current national Paralympic cycling champion. Max had flown down to Atlanta Friday afternoon to attend a track-and-field event AA had eyes on sponsoring next year. "Man," he puffed, wheezing so hard he could barely see the competitor. "You…are…fast."

Luke Sullivan looked as if he could have done another ten laps. "Six medals to prove it." He snagged the hem of his T-shirt and used it to wipe his sweating forehead. The guy looked nearly military—lean, muscular, buzz-cut hair. Max thought the guy could probably take on half of JJ's old army unit sitting down. Sullivan had just won yet another race—his third of the day. "You have some skills there—for an amateur, I mean. With a little training, you could hold your own."

Before working with Adventure Access and their sponsorship of para-athletic events around the country, Max never even knew there were professional athletes like Luke. The guy was impressive. "I'm not the dedicated type. I'll stick to the flashier side—no pesky results to worry about."

"There's flash enough on my end of the deal," Luke boasted. "You'll see at the sponsors' dinner Sunday night." He gave a knowing smirk. "Lots of ladies."

That was a business perk Alex hadn't discussed. "Shame I've got a four-o'clock flight Sunday. Remind me to stay over till Monday next time."

Luke rolled his massive shoulders and started wheeling toward the equipment trailers. "Yeah, the competition is fun, but the pity perks are outstanding."

Max caught up with him. "The what?"

"Aw, come on—you know what I mean. The rehab nurses. The physical therapists. All those *helping professionals.*" He gave the last two words a locker-room tone of voice, and Max's mild shock must have shown on his face. "You're, what, four-teen months out? Injured last summer, wasn't it?"

"July. And what's that got to do with anything?"

Luke pulled up closer. "How many dates have you had since then?"

Max suddenly wasn't interested in playing notch-on-the-post with this guy. Not that he was a long-term-relationship guy himself, but he hadn't realized a legend like Luke Sullivan took the phrase "wheel-ing womanizer" to a new level. "Enough." Was Sullivan for real? JJ lectured him on taking Heather to dinner when there were guys like *this* rolling around the world?

Luke's chuckle of disbelief annoyed Max. "Yeah, just like I thought. Not one, huh? You need to play to your strengths, Jones. Pity perks are all we get around here. Don't go believing that rehab nonsense about rich, full lives with all the same things we'd have had before the chair. We're out of that race you don't see too many of us rolling down the aisle."

Max halted his wheels, a bit stunned. Of all the guys in chairs to garner a full social life, Sullivan should top the list. "Wait a minute—you've been in a chair for, what, six years?"

"Seven and a half."

"And you're telling me no woman has ever gone out with you for just—"

Sullivan cut him off with a laugh and waved his

hand as if the thought were ludicrous. "Pity perks are all you get, dude. Best to own up to that now."

"But…"

Luke angled to face Max. "Sure, there are the ones that talk a great game. Acceptance, accessibility—oh, the social workers are really good at that one—and they'll stick with you for a little while. Then you get sick or they want to go on vacation somewhere you can't go, or worse yet, their family gets wind of it. Then it's bye-bye."

Max was sorry he could still feel enough of his gut for it to knot. "Don't mess with me. Come on, you're like G.I. Joe in a chair. If somebody like you only gets dates out of pity, what hope is there for the rest of us?"

"That's just it, dude. There isn't any hope. Don't get sucked in. In the end, you're just the compassion merit badge. And it feels like being dropped a mile. You want my advice? Don't even try to do the relationship thing. It doesn't work."

It was the first time Max had ever found anyone more cynical than himself, and it wasn't a pretty sight. "That's harsh, man."

"Better to know now. Relationships do not work out for guys like us. Let me guess—your rehab therapist told you not to start a serious relationship for the first year, right?"

Max tried to remember the speech he'd received and mostly ignored. "Well, yeah. I figured it wouldn't be all that easy, but I didn't take myself totally out of the market. I mean, there have to be women who can handle this." His thoughts went to Heather and the bright future she'd painted for Simon. She thought it possible.

"No," Luke said with a dark certainty Max practically felt run cold down the back of his neck. "Only women who *think* they can. And everybody finds out how ugly that can get." Luke pulled up to his regular chair and shifted himself out of the racing model with a strength and agility Max had to admire. The guy was the best in the world, and an Adonis on wheels to boot. If anybody knew the rules of the game, it was Luke Sullivan. "Sorry to be the bearer of grim news, but better you know now. It just isn't possible." With a bump of his fist on Max's shoulder, Luke wheeled off in the direction of the athlete's tent.

The entire concept of Adventure Access was that anything was possible for someone with a disability. Well, almost anything. Then again, Max knew that JJ had a bucketload of veteran friends whose marriages and relationships hadn't survived the injuries soldiers brought home. Granted, he hadn't been at this very long, but now that he thought about it, he hadn't run into one happily married man in a chair. He'd just figured they weren't into the sports and outdoor pursuits AA sponsored—the company had a decidedly young demographic—but what if they weren't out there at all? What if Luke was right?

Luke Sullivan, you're pretty much a jerk, aren't you? Max thought bitterly. Luke couldn't be right. The guy's paralysis just started at his heart, that was all. He'd known men who attacked their dating life with that "take no prisoners" attitude—he'd been one himself, for crying out loud. Max decided he no longer admired Luke Sullivan very much—the guy's handicap went a lot further than his legs.

Until he remembered something an old friend of his had said—one of the many friends who had fallen by the wayside, unable to cope with the new world of "Max on Wheels"—that now rang disturbingly true: *Sometimes it's the jerks who say out loud what we all wish weren't true.*

Chapter Seven

Max wasn't back in town more than twenty-four hours before JJ insisted he come with her and Alex to attend the funeral of Mort Wingate, an older guy in town who'd been sick for a while.

"I know who Mort is…was…but it's not like I was close to the guy," Max argued with JJ outside the church entrance.

"That doesn't matter," JJ retorted. "You know his daughter, Melba, and her husband, Clark, and this is as much about them as it is about Mort." JJ went all motherly on Max, an odd soft tone in her voice as she found something to brush off his shoulder. "This is how community works, Max. Everybody's there for everybody else."

His sister and her new husband had really made Gordon Falls home in a way that even he hadn't, although he'd lived there longer. In fact, JJ had been house-sitting for him when she'd first met Alex, who'd been on a sabbatical of sorts in Gordon Falls. They'd met, they'd become friends, they'd grown close…and then they'd watched it all fall apart thanks to Max's injury. Adventure Access was born from the ashes of Adventure Gear, Alex's old company that had made the new, experimental climbing line from which Max had fallen. Anger, blame and guilt had separated Alex and JJ for a time in the aftermath, but they'd worked it all out.

As for himself, Max had long stopped caring whether the injury was the result of faulty equipment or his own recklessness. JJ would say that was God's healing. To Max, it simply didn't seem worth the energy to point fingers now that all that business had been settled. Especially since Alex and JJ looked so happy that Max could almost believe the stuff JJ spouted about how God had worked that whole mess for good.

That was easy to believe when the "for good" had really changed your life "for good." Sure, his job at Adventure Access was far better than anything he'd done before the accident, but it didn't quite even out in Max's view, nor could he really believe that it would. It had all left him on not very friendly terms with God, which was why it made him so antsy to be wheeling into the Gordon Falls Community Church for this funeral.

"There's a spot for chairs up front," Alex said,

knowing Max hadn't set foot in the sanctuary despite living in Gordon Falls for nearly two years.

"Up front? Can't the newbies sit in the back?"

"What, so you can cut out early?" JJ chided. "Come on—I promise it won't hurt."

The church was packed. Max couldn't help but wonder—if he hadn't survived his fall, would his funeral have been packed the pews like this? Max mostly avoided pondering the reason why he was still here. For a few seconds there with Simon, however, he'd felt a glimmer of what he supposed Alex would call "purpose." He certainly was doing good at Adventure Access—people told him every day how he changed their perceptions of what was possible after an injury like his. That was satisfying to hear, but it wasn't the kind of thing a guy could build a life on. What Luke Sullivan did accomplished the same thing, but Max had no desire to end up a bitter, manipulative skeptic like Sullivan, even if it did mean a packed social schedule.

"You're here," Heather Browning said with a disturbing air of surprise as she walked up the church aisle. She looked over at JJ. "Can I sit with you all?"

"Sure," Max said before JJ had a chance to respond, rolling his chair back a bit to give her access to the pew next to him. Maybe church wasn't so boring, after all. When she'd settled into her seat, he leaned over and whispered, "Melba is friends with you and JJ, isn't she?"

Heather nodded. "She's had a long go of taking care of Mort. Clark, too." She motioned to where Melba; her husband, the fire chief, Clark Bradens; and some other people still stood in the back of the sanctuary. "It's so sad."

"Never seen a happy funeral."

Heather looked up. "Oh, I have."

"A happy funeral? Isn't that sort of an oxymoron?"

The organ music softened, signaling the start of the service. "Not really. I'll tell you after the service."

For a church service, Max had to admit it wasn't that bad. Heather had a sweet singing voice, so he didn't mind that he didn't know any of the songs, because it gave him a chance to listen to her. Pastor Allen wasn't half-bad for a minister type—he actually seemed pretty down-to-earth. He talked about death as heading home to a place where all the mental and physical limitations Mort had endured late in life would be gone, where he'd be reunited with his late wife, where he'd finally see the God who loved him face-to-face. Allen made it sound as if he looked forward to his time to go, even though JJ talked all the time about his family and the strength of his friendships.

When Clark stood up and read a letter Melba had written, there was barely a dry eye in the room. When a group of older woman from the church walked up and draped Mort's casket with a stunning moss-green blanket of sorts, even Max got a lump in his throat thinking of the prayer shawl the same ladies had given him. His was black with flames on it—just like his car—and while he'd never admit it to anyone, it was one of his prized possessions. Power of prayer or no, the thing always seemed to make him feel better whenever he pulled it over his lap or shoulders. The gift had been the first evidence of the Gordon Falls community he'd seen. And now Mort had been given his last. He hadn't thought that kind of stuff ever really happened anymore.

"That was beautiful, wasn't it?" Heather asked when she closed the hymnal after the final song. She wore a pretty sky-colored dress that fluttered in the breeze coming through the open church windows. The sun coming through the stained glass cast her hair in a myriad of colors. She—and Alex and JJ for that matter—looked so at home in the church where he still felt like an intruder. Or worse yet, an impostor. He couldn't seem to drum up whatever it was that Alex and JJ and now even Heather obviously got from the place.

"Yeah," he agreed, meaning it. "It was really nice. I hadn't realized all the history Mort had with the town." Max had been in a hurry to leave the Ohio suburb of his youth, and while folks had been nothing but friendly when he'd opened the boat and cabin rental business here, he hadn't felt the deep connection other people seemed to make. Not yet at least, but he could feel the edges of it starting to catch.

"Want to get some coffee and say hello? Simon and his dad are over there with Melba and Clark." Heather pointed to the large meeting room, where people were gathering and chatting.

"Max!" Simon shouted and waved. The boy's enthusiasm caught in the back of Max's throat. "I saw you earlier. Hey, guess what?"

Max wheeled up to him, offering him a fist bump and a smile that didn't need any forcing at all. "What?"

"I'm joining the Ping-Pong Club. Ms. Browning talked to the teacher and everything."

Heather's smile was wide and downright adorable. "It was Simon's idea. Mr. Jackson said yes in a heartbeat."

Simon angled up beside Max. "Bailey Morton is in the Ping-Pong Club." He said the girl's name with the flat-out hormonal fascination only high school boys could achieve.

"Cute, huh?"

Simon sighed. "Way out of my league."

"Cut that out!" Max pulled back in mock shock, then leaned in to whisper, "Don't sell yourself short. Chicks dig the wheels."

The resulting look on Simon's face was priceless—until the scowl on Mr. Williams's face shut down the conspiracy. "An academic club is a good idea for Simon, don't you think?" It was clear Mr. Williams had something closer to Math Club or Chess Club in mind.

"The way he smoked us last time, I think Simon has awesome prospects in the Ping-Pong Club." Max pointed at Simon. "I gave you my cell number last time, so you keep me posted on your progress." Just because he couldn't help himself, he winked and added, "On all fronts. Text me. Anytime."

Simon grinned. "You got it."

Heather, who had acquired two cups of coffee, nodded toward some chairs lined up along the wall. He liked that she intuitively looked for ways to get them at eye level with each other without him having to ask her to do so. Not everyone caught on to how hard it was to keep craning his neck up all the time.

"Do you even realize what you've done for that boy?" she asked, handing the cup to him as she sat down. She actually teared up a bit as she stared back at Simon, and the look in her eyes lodged sharp and sweet in Max's chest.

He didn't really know how to respond. "He's a good kid. Just…unsure, I suppose."

"He thinks the world of you. You know that."

He cleared his throat, her glistening eyes again catching him up short. "Oh, people used to think a lot of things about me and what I did, but that kind of admiration hasn't ever really entered the picture."

"It's a gift, Max. A trust, really." She cast her eyes back at Simon. "Just promise me you'll take care with it, okay?" Heather took her passion for her work to a personal level Max hadn't ever seen. It was as if these kids were her own kids; she cared that much.

"Yeah, sure. I get that." He took a sip of coffee, needing to break the intensity of the moment. "I'm choking in this tie. Let's go get some air."

Heather stepped onto the path that led from Gordon Falls Community Church down toward the town's picturesque riverbank. She'd always found nature's beauty to be the best balm for the soul after something as heavy as a funeral, and it was clear to see Max wasn't at ease inside the church.

"So," Max said as he negotiated a corner with an effortless grace, "you said you were going to tell me about a happy funeral."

"I did, didn't I?"

"I'll give you this much—Mort's did feel happier than I expected. But I'm still skeptical."

"It was my grandmother's funeral service," Heather answered. She cast her memory back to the brisk October morning when Mom had laid her extraordinary mother to rest. "She had the best funeral I've ever attended. It was like a big, thankful celebration. She even made us have cake. She said she wanted it to be like an enormous party for her graduation into heaven. She was an amazing woman, my Grannie Annie."

Max eyebrow shot up at the name. "Grannie Annie? Really?"

Grannie Annie would have had a field day with the jaded look in Max's eyes. "Oh, she was a great lady. I hope I'm just like her at that age—she lived until she was eighty-seven and sharp as a tack all the way until the end. Mom used to say Grannie Annie squeezed every drop out of life every day." Heather hugged her chest, Grannie Annie's musical voice and lively eyes coming to mind. "If it weren't for her help after my accident, I don't know how I'd ever have made it through."

Max put out a hand to stop her walking. "How were you burned? Where?" He motioned to the stone wall that ran along the sidewalk. "I mean, if you're okay with telling me."

She wasn't. She wasn't ever really comfortable with telling anyone about that year—it let people in too close once they knew. Still, Max had told her about his own injury; it didn't seem fair to hold out just because it was hard. She swallowed.

"It looks like you've made a fine recovery, but I have no business prying if you don't want to talk about it. I of all people get how that feels."

"No, it just…it's hard to talk about. Exactly because I look fine. I mean I feel fine, but…well, *recovery* doesn't really seem to be the right word." The words weren't coming, so she decided it was easier to show him. She walked over to the low wall he'd pointed out, satisfied it wasn't in wide view, and sat down. Max wheeled over next to her. With a deep breath, Heather lifted the long hem of her skirt to just above her left knee, where the scars started.

She was glad he didn't say anything. He didn't do that awful sucking in of breath, that unedited reaction she imagined most people would have to the nasty visual of her scarred leg. She let the hem fall back, suddenly aware of all the feeling that had left that part of her body. The swath of numb, tough scar tissue and skin graft the doctors had called such a victory. Most days she was grateful—she knew lots of other burn patients who had it far worse and she still had a fair amount of mobility in that hip. Other days she felt damaged and discarded no matter how much her faith told her otherwise.

"What did that to you?" he said softly.

"Oil."

"That sounds awful. I'm sorry."

Did he realize he'd just said the very thing he disliked other people saying about his accident? He sounded sincere, and she was glad he didn't try to crack a joke. There weren't jokes to make about this, ever.

"I worked at a fried-chicken place in high school.

One night a drunk driver—a senior from my own school, in fact—plowed through the front windows. Lots of people were hurt, and while no one lost their lives, I was standing in front of the deep fryers when they…" She never could quite come up with the right verb for what had happened. But the sound? The glass crunching and people screaming and the horrible hissing before she blacked out? She could describe that down to the last terrible detail.

"I woke up in a burn unit with all kinds of patches and pads and drugs dripping into IVs. I missed most of my junior year between all the surgeries and infections, but I walked down the aisle to get my diploma."

"Your grandmother took care of you?"

"Not the way you'd think. My mom saw to most of my care. My dad, well, he didn't handle the whole thing well. He wanted to see somebody pay for ruining his precious little girl, and he sort of let that crusade swallow him whole. Grannie Annie found ways to keep me happy, to keep me from making my whole life about my left leg."

Max was quiet for a long time before he said, "I was your dad, at first. I let my accident swallow me for a while. I wanted someone to pay." He wasn't siding with her dad; he was confessing his own downward spiral. "You might have read about it in the papers. I wasn't exactly keeping a low profile."

She nodded, the lump in her throat too big to let

words past. She knew he'd been bitter. JJ had told her some of it, and Max had managed to get himself into the papers and the media for a variety of less-than-healthy behaviors in the early months after his accident. It was what had kept her from calling Max to help with Simon in the first place. She realized, looking at him now, that she'd projected a lot of her dad onto Max because of how they'd both reacted to a tragedy. The men in her life until now had left her with scars and numbness in places Max couldn't see. She'd vowed to only let people into her life who fought against bitterness, not those who succumbed to it. She wasn't completely sure yet which of those Max Jones was.

"Where are your mom and dad now?"

She picked a small stone up from the path beside her feet and fiddled with it. "They split up my sophomore year in college. Dad couldn't put the battle-ax down and Mom couldn't heal both him and me at the same time. I spent the summer of my freshman year home from college at Grannie Annie's because they were fighting so much by then."

"What happened to the guy who hit the store?"

Oh, that was the million-dollar question, the thing that had turned Dad into the person he became—and in some ways had turned her into the person she became. "Not enough, really. He had rich, powerful parents who hired supersmart lawyers. They managed to pull in a question of mechanical failure despite the guy's blood-alcohol level. Eventually, he pleaded into a deal that got him out in no time. I think that's what got to Dad most of all." Heather dared a look up into Max's face. All the smart aleck was gone. Just the intensity of his eyes was left, warm where they had been defensive. She touched her left leg. "I got the life sentence and he got off easy. Hard to swallow, if you know what I mean."

"I'm sorry." It was almost a whisper, and Max looked down at his hands for a moment. "I'm sorry, and that isn't useless, is it?"

Something unfurled in Heather's defenses. A tiny piece of her—one that had started blooming larger at the Ping-Pong match—dared to believe that maybe Max wasn't here by mistake. Maybe Max was exactly who Simon needed.

And maybe more than just Simon.

Chapter Eight

"You were really good in there." Alex grinned as he and Max got into the elevator after an important work presentation Wednesday morning.

"Thanks." Max pushed the button for the ground floor. "They weren't too hard a crowd to win over."

"Maybe so, and you know persuasion is a specialty of mine, but I don't think we'd have gotten that much buy-in to the concept if you weren't in the room. I'm still just the guy with the good idea, but you're the guy who proves it works." Alex leaned back against the elevator wall. "I'm glad you're on board. Just saying." After a second he added, "Do you miss the boat biz?"

Max's boat and cottage rental business in Gordon Falls had barely been getting by when he was injured. Now JJ mostly ran it—and ran it well—when she wasn't at the volunteer fire department. "I can still dip my toes back in the water when I need to.

And I've got the *Sea Legs,* which is more fun than my desk any day. Besides, the business is doing better under your wife's management than it ever did under mine. She's an outstanding employee."

Alex raised an eyebrow. "I thought JJ was a full partner now."

She was. "I just get a kick out of calling her an employee. She's not anymore, but, you know, I just can't seem to remember that." Max tapped his head. "Blocked neural pathways or something."

"Uh-huh." Alex checked his watch. "I've got another meeting at two, but you want to grab some lunch? There was a café in the lobby and presentations always make me hungry."

Max noticed a familiar look in Alex's eyes. The one that signaled "a conversation." Trouble was, Max hadn't quite figured out if the look meant a brother-in-law conversation or an employee conversation. "Sure, I could eat. If I can get in there okay."

"I scoped it out on the way in," Alex admitted, which told Max this meal wasn't as spontaneous as it had sounded. "You'll be fine." Most places in larger cities and towns, that was true—the world was becoming a more accessible place every day. But Gordon Falls and other historic small towns still held their share of challenges. The Gordon Falls Community Church hadn't had a decent wheelchair ramp until last year.

"So," Alex said carefully once they'd settled in with a pair of hefty sandwiches, "JJ is worried about you."

Max snickered. "JJ's always worried about me."

"Let me rephrase that." Alex pinched the bridge of his nose. "JJ is worried about you and Heather Browning."

"I've already been given the full speech, Alex." Max rolled his eyes. "I don't need it from you, too."

"Hey." Alex put up his hands. "I'm actually on your side here. But you know JJ. Friendships are hard for her, and she is worried you'll mess things up with Heather. You can't blame her, given your previous track record."

"I haven't dated anyone since the accident. I've been a very good little injured boy." His words had a little more edge than was perhaps necessary, but this was a sore spot. "If I wanted to be mothered, I'd have moved back to Ohio." Max ripped open his bag of chips. "Go arrange for JJ to meet Luke Sullivan. The guy's a predator on wheels. Gave me a really *inspirational* speech about the leverage of pity when scoring with the ladies. You can tell JJ she has nothing to worry about from me."

The look of surprise on Alex's face was satisfying. People held Sullivan up as a beacon of inspiration. Max had half a mind to let a few things slip to the media about what a boor the guy really was, only he didn't have the heart to shoot any bad press toward Paralympic sports.

"Charming. Remind me to take him off my list of potential spokespersons. Just proves there can a jerk factor in any business, hmm?" Alex took a bite, but he was still forming a conversation—Max could see the next question percolating behind his boss's eyes. "So you want to tell me what exactly *is* going on between you and Heather? I saw you walking out of the church service with her, and that was a pretty wide grin you were wearing for a guy who just got dragged into a funeral."

Max still hadn't decided how much he wanted to get into this with Alex. "I get a kick out of helping her help Simon. You ought to understand how that feels."

"Oh, I do. I get that. But Simon wasn't out on the riverbank for half an hour with you. And Simon hasn't prompted you to ditch dinner with us—well, not yet anyway. I'm glad you showed that night, but it would have helped if you hadn't outlawed any conversation regarding Heather at dinner. JJ thinks you're hiding something from her. You know how she gets." Alex pointed at Max with the straw of his soda. "*Are* you hiding a relationship with Heather?"

Max put his sandwich down hard enough to tumble the bread off one side. "I do not have a relationship with Heather Browning."

Alex was fully engaged now, in that communication mode that made him an unstoppable force. "Do you *want* a relationship with Heather Browning?"

Just because he needed to stall, Max said, "Is that really any of your business if I do?"

"Not at all. But I'm going to ask anyway. She's not really what I'd pick as your type."

"I like her." He felt safe admitting that—JJ had probably already guessed that much. "Only the timing is way off."

"Sort of." Given the terrible timing of Alex and JJ's meeting, the argument didn't hold much weight with Alex. "Maybe not, if she's really special."

"To tell you the truth, I'd be better if I liked her a little less, because I'm not quite sure how to…do this whole thing…on wheels, that is. In case you haven't noticed, I come with a whole lot of extra baggage now."

"Everybody's got baggage. Yours is just easier to see."

Alex's words brought the image of Heather's scarred leg to mind. She was still among the walking wounded, only no one saw her pain or recognized her fear. "I can barely cope with all the stuff involved in my condition. How am I supposed to ask someone else to take it on?"

"What if she's strong enough to take it on?" Alex sat back in his chair. "Look at how she champions Simon Williams's cause. I think if anyone could make it work, it'd be someone like her."

He couldn't help but think of Sullivan's words, *They only think they can.* "I don't want to get far into this and find out it won't work. I'd like to think I'm done with breaking ladies' hearts." That was only half-true; a tiny newfound part of him was worried it was *his* heart that would end up broken. He'd been dumped for being a jerk so many times it had almost become a painless game. The thought of someone—especially someone like Heather— breaking it off with him not because he was a jerk, but because of his broken body? That was too harsh to risk. Sullivan was right about one thing: Heather would try so hard to make it work that it would go all the way to the bitter end before she'd admit she wasn't up to the challenge.

"You know," Alex suggested, emphasizing his point with a pickle spear, "you could try something totally un-Max here."

"What would that be?"

"Go slow."

"Ha. Funny."

"This may be exactly what you need. Have you ever thought about that? You can't slam through the gears on this one. You have to take it one little bit at a time. That's completely new territory for you. In a lot of ways."

Max couldn't decide if having Alex in favor of this relationship—and it wasn't a relationship yet— was a good thing or a bad thing. Alex was staring at him with narrow, assessing eyes, as if he were some kind of puzzle to solve, some new project to tackle. The scrutiny was a little unnerving.

"You really like her, don't you?"

Max decided he couldn't fight Alex, JJ, Brian Williams and gravity all at the same time. "Yeah," he admitted. "There's something about her. She sticks with me even when I don't want her to, you know?"

Alex gave him a wily smile. "Yeah, I do know how that feels. When do you see her next?"

Max tried to keep the anticipation from his voice. "Tonight, but it's school business."

"That's good. Go slow. But keep me posted."

Well, Heather thought as she pulled up to the address Max had given her, *at least I know why he said to bring gloves and a sweater.* The parking lot of the County Ice Arena was full for a Wednesday night in September, but she had no trouble picking out a certain boxy black car in one of the handicapped parking spaces.

"Are we watching hockey?" she asked Max as he met her at the door.

He dismissed her question with a wave, rolling into the building. "Nah. Girls don't like hockey."

"I know many *women* who enjoy a good hockey game." She couldn't tell if he persisted with using *girl* because he forgot she didn't like it or because he remembered her irritation.

"But you're not one of them, are you?" His eyes held a bit of mischief.

"Actually, no. Which brings me back to my original question. What are we doing here?"

"That's not your original question." Max held up a correcting finger as he swerved his chair around a corner past the skate rental booth. "Your original question was are we watching hockey. No, we are not watching hockey. We are *playing* hockey."

Heather stopped walking.

Max noticed and swiveled around. "Kiddie-sitting-down hockey, actually. Okay, well, the technical name is sled hockey, but c'mon, a five-year-old could do this. You'll be fine. And then you can give Brian Williams a firsthand account of how Simon will survive intact when he joins us next time."

Heather didn't see how hockey, a sport famous for erupting in tooth-shattering fistfights, would pass the Brian Williams safety standards. Still, she followed Max around to the far corner of the rink, where a section had been cordoned off with a pair of goals and some devices that did indeed look like sleds. A pair of miniature hockey sticks—not more than a foot high—sat in each of the sleds. "You're serious."

Max wheeled past a rink employee, giving the man a high five as he rolled by. "Thanks, Henry."

"Anytime, Max." Henry looked up and gave Heather an enthusiastic but toothless smile. "Hiya, sweetie."

"Hello there." Heather tried to make her wave casual, but it ended up feeling more like a hyperactive flailing than any kind of greeting.

Henry put his hands on his hips. "You ain't never done this before, have you? Look at you—you're a tiny thing, aren't ya?" He chuckled. "This ought to be fun to watch."

"Cut it out, Henry. This is professional. Ms. Browning is from the high school and we're looking at recreational options for a student."

Heather's eyebrows shot up at the formal choice of vocabulary. While his words were professional, Max's expression was decidedly personal.

"Uh-huh." Henry's skepticism was hard to miss. "That's right." He grinned again and pointed at Heather. "You watch out for him, now. He's a tricky one."

"I've caught on to that," Heather replied. "Exactly how does this work?"

Max zipped up the fleece jacket he wore—she hadn't noticed until now that it bore the emblem of Chicago's NHL team, the Blackhawks—and pulled a pair of gloves from the pockets. "Pretty much the way it looks. Only getting into the sled might be a touch easier for you than it is for me." With no more explanation than that, Max rolled his chair out onto a ramped section of carpeting laid out next to the two sleds. With the same athletic prowess she'd seen at their first meeting, he maneuvered himself out of the chair and into the long, low sled, lifting his legs into place. "There are usually special gloves and helmets, but we're not going to get that complicated today. I'll show them to you, though, so you can report back to Mr. Williams on the abundance of safety equipment. Come on—get in." He motioned to the second sled as he began strapping his legs in place.

Max was right; it was pretty obvious how the whole setup worked. Given what a terrible skater she was in the standing position, this felt slightly less perilous—if one ignored the Max element of any activity. She buckled the strap that went over her lap and pulled on her gloves. "Like this?"

"You know—" Max grinned "—I never thought I'd use the word *cute* in a hockey setting. Watch the other end of the sticks. They've got little teeth on them."

"Why?"

"So you can do this." With a trick worthy of a rock-and-roll drummer, he twirled the sticks in the air and then sunk them into the ice so that the teeth gripped. Then he pushed off and went sliding down the rink toward the goal at the other end.

Heather took a breath, set her sticks on either side of her and pushed. It wasn't as hard as she thought to send her sled across the ice, and she found it much more fun to be daring without the constant fear of falling. They played politely at first, gently skidding the soft, light puck back and forth. As her comfort and ability increased, the game dissolved into a fun frenzy of yelling and cheering, egging each other on to spectacular shots and daring defenses. Each goal scored—and she managed to score her fair share—took the game to a new exuberance...until she tipped over after attempting to cut off Max's shot at the goal.

"Watch your hands," Max said, a bit out of breath as he pulled up next to her, facing the opposite direction. "Give me one arm and I'll help you up."

The rescue brought him precariously close, their shoulders touching as he gripped her upper body to upright the sled. Once up, they were facing each other at very close range. Heather looked up and got an unsettlingly close look at his eyes. They were an intriguing hazel—not quite brown, but neither gray nor green, either. They fit his personality—expressive, unclassifiable and a bit dark around the edges. She'd always thought of him as physically strong, but today Heather *felt* that strength. He lifted her as if she were a feather.

Max pulled off one glove, reached up and brushed some ice flakes off her cheek. His touch fluttered through her, her breath short from more than just the marvelous energy of the game. Heather grew warm despite the rink's chill. He was attractive in a perilous sort of way, knowing what she knew about him. JJ had bemoaned Max's past trail of broken hearts, and right now she could see why a woman would believe anything he said up this close. From a distance he was all flash and sharp edges, but this proximity offered Heather a glimpse of something completely different. She saw a jumbled man just trying to figure out how to put his life back together. Wondering, seeking, cautious behind all his cavalier bravado. He was much easier to dismiss from a distance, but so magnetic up close.

He did not move his fingers from where they brushed her cheek. He did not take his grip from her shoulder. He didn't back off one tiny bit. "You okay?" he asked, his voice quiet and rough.

That was the real question, wasn't it? Being so near to him felt both nice and precarious at the same time. He understood her, accepted things about her other people couldn't hope to understand. And yet she wasn't ready to trust him to keep those things safe and unharmed. "I just lost my balance for a moment." It was true in more ways than one.

"But you're okay?"

"Fine." Her answer came out as more of a squeak than a word.

"Liar." She wasn't anything close to fine, and they both knew it. He took his hand from her cheek, and she felt the loss in more than the rush of cold air against her skin. "I don't…know…what to do here. I'm not sure where this goes, or if it goes anywhere. My balance is sort of…off, too, if you know what I mean."

"I do."

"JJ doesn't want me anywhere near you. Outside of school, that is."

Heather managed a nervous laugh. "She told me I should steer clear of you. That you would try something and I shouldn't fall for it."

He became the little brother just then, embarrassed by his big sister, his smirk disarming. "You fell all by yourself there, kiddo." There was a spot on his own hair where flakes of ice from their scuffle had settled like snow, and she longed to reach out and brush it off. She wondered whether his wavy hair was soft or coarse. He finally broke his gaze and looked down, fiddling with one of the strap buckles on the sled. "I'm still figuring out how all this goes together. I used to be…well, let's just say JJ had good reason to warn you off. I just don't know if all this—" he waved his hand over his legs "—makes it better or worse, or even if it's possible."

"Of course it's possible." She replied so fast it rang like a platitude. Suddenly it felt like both the right answer and the wrong answer. "I mean, you should be—"

"Please." A bit of the edge returned to his voice as he cut her off. "I can't bear to hear the 'full and happy life' speech. Not from you." His bitterness pushed all the warmth from the air between them.

"It's more complicated, but that doesn't make it impossible."

Max eased their sleds apart. "Alex would tell you climbing Mount Everest is complicated but not impossible, but that doesn't mean everyone should do it."

Chapter Nine

Max tried to "go slow," staying away from school for the next two days, not returning until his next meeting with Simon after school Friday. They played one-on-one basketball and talked about the prospects of hockey.

In the parking lot after the game, Simon tried on one of the hockey gloves Max had given him to test. "How'd it happen?"

Max looked up from the sled he was putting into his van. He'd brought it to show Simon, hoping it would further convince him to come play hockey sometime soon. Simon was clearly interested, but with ice, sharp blades and the potential for aggressive play, it was going to be an uphill battle with Mr. Williams. "How'd I get my dashing good looks?"

"No." Simon looked sheepish. "You know…"

Max pushed the sled fully into the van and turned

to face Simon. He was surprised it had taken Simon this long to ask. "You mean how'd I get my wheels?"

"Yeah. You haven't ever told me about your accident."

Handing him the other glove of the pair, Max hit the button that shut the van door. "You haven't asked me. I figured when you wanted to know, you'd ask." He looked at Simon. Once the kid's face grew into those big blue eyes and he grew his hair out a little longer, Simon could swing some serious charm. Despite the shyness, the boy was genuinely curious about things, and that made him a good listener. "It doesn't have to be the first thing everyone knows about you, you know. It's a part of you—a big part—but not all of you."

They wheeled together to the stretch of grass beside the school parking lot. "I always see it in people's eyes, you know?" Simon said. "Like they need to ask but think I'll be upset if they do." He shrugged. "I'm kinda used to my condition—it's not like it's a whole new tragedy or anything."

Whole new tragedy. Max was sick enough of people referring to what happened to him as "a tragedy." What must a lifetime of that feel like? People usually experienced cerebral palsy from birth, so it wasn't as if Simon knew anything different, but still. No one's life should be branded a tragedy. Not anyone who was fifteen, at least. "That's why I like little kids," Max offered. "They just ask you what they want to know, right out."

Simon nodded. "Then their parents get all freaky and shush them."

Max rolled his eyes. "Tell me about it. Happened to me the other day at Karl's. Right in front of Heath…Ms. Browning."

That made Simon's eyes pop. "How do you get into Karl's?"

Like any coffee shop anywhere, Karl's was a favorite high school hangout. It stuck in Max's gut that Simon considered it off-limits. He leaned in toward the boy. "You ring the bell at the back door and Karl lets you in through the kitchen. Then he gets you the corner table 'cause it's the only place guys like you and I fit. Anybody he has to move gets a free coffee, so everybody wins. You and I should go sometime. I'll show you the ropes."

Simon looked as if that would make his week, much less his day. "Man, I'd like that." He looked down, fiddling with one of the gloves. "So you and Ms. Browning, huh?"

Max was an idiot for thinking it wouldn't come to this at some point. "Well, I don't know yet. We're sort of trying to figure it out."

Simon laughed. "What's to figure out? She's a girl. She's pretty."

"She's the school counselor and I'm kind of here in an official capacity. Plus, things are kind of tricky in the dating department for those of us of the wheeled persuasion." Remembering Luke Sullivan, Max felt compelled to add, "Not impossible, just different." He gave Simon a companionable nudge to the arm of his chair. "So, who do you like?"

Simon actually blushed. Max suddenly felt a hundred years old, all mentor-ish and falsely wise. "Well, there's Bailey."

"Oh, from the Ping-Pong Club, right?"

"Yeah." Simon angled to face Max and moaned, "Only, it's like all she can see is the chair, you know?"

Max put his elbows on his knees, leaning in like a two-man football huddle. "So you gotta show her the great guy *in* the chair. I won't lie to you—it'll take time and some serious charm, but I think you're up to it."

"A guy like you, maybe."

"And a guy like you. Don't count yourself out of the running just because you roll. That's what I always say."

"Are you in the running with Ms. Browning?"

"I should tell you that such a question is none of your business." The statement got the "yeah, right" look from Simon that Max would have expected. "But the truth is I'm trying to keep it strictly official with Ms. Browning for reasons that don't have anything to do with you and me or school."

"Like what?" Simon was not going to let him get away with an avoidance like that.

How could he explain this on a level a fifteen-year-old would understand? Max took the sunglasses off the top of his head and folded them into his shirt pocket just to buy himself time to think. "You, you've been in a chair your whole life, right? None of that is new for you. The high school part is new, but not the chair part. Me, I'm still figuring out the chair part. Everything I thought I wanted from life is a bit different now. Some of it's better, some of it not so much. At first, I thought they were being jerks down at the hospital when they told me not to get into any serious relationships for a year. Now I think maybe that's not such bad advice."

"And you think if you got into it with Ms. Browning, it'd get serious?"

Well, now, that was pretty perceptive for a fifteen-year-old. It *would* get serious—fast—if he "got into it" with Heather. And while he'd tell anyone it was to spare Heather any heartbreak, some still-wounded little part of him was out-and-out terrified it'd be *his* heart lying shredded on the ground when she walked away. "I think that's a question we won't get to answer." Just to change the subject, he pointed at Simon. "Hey, wait a minute. This was supposed to be the hair-raising story of my spinal cord's untimely demise, not a romance novel. And why don't you already know this one? Didn't you read about me in the papers?"

The boy smirked. "Well, I looked you up on the internet, if that's what you're asking."

"So you know the basics. I let the cameras on *Wide Wild World* get to me and I got stupid. I rappelled down that cliff face a lot faster than I ought to have 'cause I wanted to look cool. I took a lot less care than was smart 'cause I thought I was invincible. The show used gear they weren't supposed to—stuff that hadn't finished going through the testing phases—and the people who ought to have been paying attention weren't. There was a lot of finger-pointing afterward—lots of it by me, to be honest—but none of that matters much now. Plenty of blame to go around, if you know what I'm saying, but my spine didn't really care who whacked it against that scaffold."

"Did it hurt?"

It was the question everyone always asked, which he found funny, since the result of his injury was that he could no longer feel. "Probably. I don't remember the actual fall or any of the next day. I've seen the fall—they had it on tape, since it was TV—but I've only watched it once." That had been a mistake. His doctors had advised against it, but he'd found he couldn't resist once he knew the tape existed. Still, Max would have rather not had that image of his flopping, twisting body burned into his memory like that. It was one of the few things in life he truly regretted. "Not really something I want to relive, you know. But once I was awake and aware of the world again, did it hurt? Not in the way you'd think. Not the 'ouch' kind of pain." He thumped a fist to his heart. "Pain comes in more ways than one, huh?"

"Yeah. I get that." Commiseration darkened Simon's features, and his eyes flicked down to the gloves for a moment. "Do you think about it? A lot, I mean?"

"My accident?" Max got the sense that wasn't Simon's real question.

"No, just…do you think…about…like what it would be like if it never happened?"

Simon wasn't asking how; Simon was asking why. Big stuff. Max wished Heather were there, thinking she was better positioned to answer those kinds of questions. Then again, who better than he? He shifted uncomfortably under the unsettling notion that Simon hadn't come into his life by accident. "All the time, buddy. All the time."

Simon looked relieved. Max remembered the firestorm of doubts that plagued any teenager, and his heart twisted for the kid.

"The thing is, everybody thinks like that. Sure, yours and my what-ifs are a little bigger and more dramatic, but every single person wonders why things happen the way they did. Alex wonders why his company crashed the way it did. Melba Bradens wonders why her dad got so sick. JJ wonders why some people died over in Afghanistan and others came away fine." He felt way out of his depth when the notion came to him to add, "It's why people go to church. To figure that stuff out."

"I haven't seen you in church other than the funeral. Do you go?"

JJ would be snickering right now if she were there. Just the other night she'd tried the ploy of "Simon is looking up to you" to get him back to church. Max hedged. "Not as much as I should."

Simon took on a mischievous smile. "Our youth group has a Friends Night next week. You should come."

Max was glad to have a way to dodge that one. "Do I look like a high school student to you?"

Simon's smile turned smug. "It's not for students. We're supposed to bring an adult we admire." The kid's eyes fairly proclaimed, *Back out of that one—I dare you.*

Nailed. JJ would howl with laughter when he told her. "You'll be sorry when I steal all your dates."

"Ha! Not a chance." A car horn sounded from the parking lot. "Mom's here. I'll text you the info."

"Show her the gloves," Max called as Simon

wheeled toward the opening van door. "And the website I told you about."

Simon gave Max a thumbs-up as he spun his chair onto the van ramp. The kid had the most irresistible smile. Who knew the scrawny little nerd would get to him like that?

Heather's heart did an unsettling little flip when Max's number came up on her desk phone. They'd both stuck strictly to email since that afternoon at the ice rink, although he'd taken to suggesting several ideas for Simon and forwarding articles he'd found at work. Did he realize how invested he'd become in Simon?

Did he have any idea how much his investment charmed her? Heather had tried so hard not to like Max Jones, and he'd managed to tear down every objection she had. More than once in her prayer journal, Max's name had been written down under the things for which she gave thanks.

She smiled as she held the receiver to her ear. "Hi there, Max."

"You've gotta help me. I don't know how to get out of this one."

The possible circumstances of Max Jones in trouble was a pretty wide world. "Out of what?"

"Youth group."

That sounded like a good story. Heather leaned back in her chair, wrapping the handset's cord around her finger. "I'll need more details than that to offer assistance." The Williamses went to GFCC just like she did, so she could guess what all this was about. She was even an adviser to the youth group. Still, she wanted to hear Max's explanation.

"Evidently there's this thing at church where kids bring friends. Adult friends. Simon sort of invited me."

Heather felt herself smile. "Congratulations. It's a big honor to be invited to Friends Night at GFCC."

There was a pause on the other end of the line. "This isn't really my thing. I don't…you know…*go* to church."

He really was worked up about it. "JJ said you used to."

"I also used to drink chocolate milk, but I don't do that anymore since my voice changed." Another pause. "I don't want to let Simon think I'm something I'm not."

"It's Friends Night, Max, not Deep Spiritual Advisers night. There isn't a test at the end. There's cake, if I remember correctly." After a second, she softened her voice to add, "You should go."

No reply.

"It'd be good for both of you." Heather sat up to lean on her desk. "You still believe in God, don't you?" Because that sounded like such a loaded question, she added, "You haven't gone off and joined some kind of creepy cult that lures in impressionable young men in wheelchairs?"

The tone of his voice changed. "Well, yeah. I mean the God part, not the creepy-cult part. I just… Look, I don't think I'm the churchy Friends Night type. I'll look…dumb. They probably all wear sweater vests and do crosswords and knitting."

She was sure Max was kidding. Mostly. "Max, your sister and brother-in-law go to that church. I go to that church. All three of us have been invited to Friends Night at one time or another, and there's not a crossword or a sweater vest among us. Although there is some knitting—which reminds me, can you meet me at the church on Tuesday at ten? There's someone I'd like you to meet. And she's *definitely* not whatever it is you think 'church ladies' are like."

"That sounds like institutionalist propaganda to me." The edge was finally gone from his voice.

"I'll buy you pie afterward. At Karl's. If you survive the trauma, that is. I'm pretty sure one of the kids invited Violet to Friends Night, so now after this you'll know someone else."

"And if I hate it?"

No one in Gordon Falls hated Violet Sharpton. It wasn't humanly possible. "If you hate it—which you won't—I'll help you get out of Friends Night with Simon. Deal?"

"Ms. Browning, you drive a hard bargain."

"And you drive a minivan with a flame paint job." It was fun to banter with him. She hadn't felt this playful in a long time.

"Don't you call my wicked-cool Honda a mini-van."

"Goodbye, Max."

"So long, counselor. Keep those teen herds of raging hormones in line."

He signed off, and she laughed. She was beginning to really enjoy the continual surprise that was Max Jones.

Chapter Ten

Max didn't make it to the church until ten-fifteen. He wasn't in a rush to meet whoever it was Heather thought he ought to meet. Just outside the church door, Max tried one last stalling tactic. "This is a dumb idea."

Heather and Melba Bradens—Heather had evidently brought reinforcements so he'd be outnumbered—crossed their hands over their chests like a pair of clucking mothers. "No, it's not. It's sweet," Heather said.

"It'd be fun for the knitters to meet you. And besides, I've had a lousy eight days, so you have to humor me." Melba yanked the door open. "Griever's choice." She walked through the doors.

Max looked at Heather. "Did she really just say 'griever's choice'?"

Heather cocked her head to one side. "Just humor her, okay? The way I hear it, you used to be the kind of guy who rushed into a room full of women."

"Ladies' night on Rush Street is one thing. The old ladies' church knitting circle is quite another."

"Melba's invited JJ and me to join," Heather teased. "We're not old ladies."

JJ had mentioned something about learning to knit. Max had visions of chunky ski hats in scary colors and scarves that itched. Still, he had to admit the black-with-flames prayer-blanket thing this group had made him was pretty cool. Regardless, Max was sure he was rolling into one of the most regrettable hours of his life.

"Ladies, I want you to meet Max Jones."

A chorus of hellos greeted him from a circle of women—remarkably, not all of them old and quite a few he recognized—sitting in the church parlor and knitting.

"Max Jones. Hot Wheels—isn't that what they call you?" A sparkly-eyed older woman he vaguely recognized aimed a pointy stick at him. "I knit your prayer shawl, honey. Had fun with it, too. Only I don't suppose you call it a shawl, now, do you?"

"I don't call it much of anything," he replied, liking her immediately despite his earlier resistance. "Except maybe warm and fuzzy."

"Violet did an amazing job, didn't she?"

"Warm and fuzzy but black with flames," she boasted. "That was a pretty tall order." He wheeled over and offered her a handshake, pleased when she didn't hesitate for a moment. "Violet Sharpton. I'm afraid I don't have a nifty nickname like yourself, but Violet's done me right all these years, so I can't complain." Violet winked at Melba. "You weren't kidding. He really is a looker."

Max withdrew his hand and decided maybe this was a dumb idea after all. "Thanks. I mean for the blanket thing. It matches my car and everything."

"Hard to miss that car," said a slightly younger woman Max remembered seeing around the firehouse. "Chad's made a few jokes about needing to douse it." The remark told him that must be Jeannie Owens, the fire marshal's wife, who ran the candy shop. More than a few baskets of her sweets had ended up in his hospital room.

"I'm rather surprised you came back to Gordon Falls, son." The oldest of the group eyed him over her glasses. "Kind of quiet for the likes of you, isn't it?"

"JJ and Alex are here. My job is nearby. There wasn't a reason to leave." Max dared a quick look at Heather. "Besides, the people are nice."

His quick glance did not go unnoticed. The old lady darted her eyes back and forth between Heather and Max, making a host of assumptions that showed on her face. "So they are."

"Stop it, Marge," Violet chimed in, swatting the assuming lady's hand. She returned her attention to Max, still boasting a knowing smile. "Marge and I got free coffee off of you two coming into Karl's the other day." She turned to the group. "Did you know Karl gives you a free drink if he has to move you so Max can have the corner table?"

Another woman looked up from her knitting. "Why don't we all go over to Karl's after this, sit in the corner table and then Max can come in? We'll all get free coffee."

Jeannie Owens laughed. "That's our Tina. Always looking for a bargain."

These weren't like any old knitting ladies in rocking chairs Max had ever met. "I don't think it works that way. Since I owe you, however, how about I bring you a pie one of these days? A payment for the blanket."

"Oh, we don't accept payment," Marge said. "And I saw in a magazine that it can be called a 'throw.'" Her eyes lit up. "Hey, that means it's a 'flame throw.' Isn't there something called a flame throw?"

Jeannie, who had barely stopped, erupted into laughter again. "That's a flamethrow*er,* Marge. If you had a teenage son with a video-game system, you'd know these kinds of things."

Violet nudged Marge in the elbow. "There is a handsome man offering to bring us pie and you're discouraging him? Did you take your pills this morning?"

"You here to learn to knit?" Tina looked a bit too pleased at the prospect.

Thankfully, Melba stepped in. "I just wanted to

make sure you got to meet Max and he got to meet you." She looked at Max. "We don't always get to meet the recipients of our prayer shawls, and you have to admit, yours was pretty special."

"JJ loves hers," Max felt compelled to offer. "My mom, too. It was a really nice thing to do."

"You're a really nice young man for saying so," Violet said. "If you'd like to learn, come in anytime. Melba taught most of us, so we like beginners."

Max didn't think his image could withstand the addition of yarn and needles. "I think I'll stick to bringing you pie."

"Maybe we can start up a club at the high school," Heather offered.

"We can look into it," Melba said. After a second, she added, "I need a new project."

Violet immediately wrapped Melba in a giant hug. "Oh, we know you do, dear. How are you holding up?"

"I'm okay," Melba said, sinking down onto the couch and grabbing a tissue from the box on the coffee table.

Heather caught Max's eye. "How about Max and I get going and leave you to the yarn and such?"

Melba looked up from dabbing her eyes. "Thanks for stopping in. Heather, I mean it about you joining."

"Once summer comes, I'm yours. You only got me this morning because parent-teacher conferences are tomorrow." She picked her handbag up off the chair where she'd laid it to run her hands through the pile of fluffy shawls. "These aren't hard to make, really?"

"Not unless you want one like Max's. The ordinary ones are just knit and purl, and even my granddaughter has learned how to do that much."

"Thanks again, ladies." Max was surprised to find out how much he truly meant it. He'd never met people this warm and friendly in the city. For all the architectural obstacles it threw in his way, Gordon Falls was worth the effort.

As Max chuckled and turned out the door, Violet called, "See you around, Hot Wheels!" He heard her voice continue from the room behind him as the door closed. "Hot Wheels. It's just too much fun to say that. I think I want a nickname."

"Violet will be there for Friends Night. She's been invited to every one, I think," Heather offered as she and Max left the church building. "She's a fabulous role model for the kids."

Max cast a glance back at the church door. "She's certainly not like any grandmother I've ever met. That's one spunky lady."

"She reminds me a lot of my Grannie Annie. Only Grannie Annie was a little softer around the edges. More the home-baked-cookies, cuddle-on-the-couch type rather than Violet's brand of high-voltage." She raised an eyebrow at Max. "You two might become great friends, you know. She's got a bit of the rebel in her, and she's taken to you—that's for sure." Max got an odd look on his face at that remark. "What?"

He brushed her concern off, busying himself with something on one of his wheels.

Heather stepped in front of him. "No, really, Max, what? Did I say something wrong?"

"No. It's not that. It's just…well, you're gonna think this is stupid. Only I can't help looking at Violet and wondering how I might have turned out with someone like her in my life. Mom didn't know what to do with me. Dad just found me disappointing. And my grandma? She was too irritated with the rest of the world to even pay attention. I don't know why I just invited myself to such an all-out pity party, but…"

It made so much sense. Max would hardly be the first person to develop an over-the-top personality just because it was the only way to get anyone in his family to notice him. JJ hadn't ever talked about her family much, only how her father's military career made it hard for him to understand JJ's difficulties serving in combat. "Your dad was quite the commander, wasn't he?"

He started heading for his car again. "We didn't call him 'General Jones' for nothing. I wore my hair long in high school just because it drove him nuts. To say we didn't get along would be putting it mildly."

"That's why you care so much about the way Simon's father treats him, isn't it?"

That earned her a sharp look. "You're not going all counselor on me now, are you? I've got a menu of shrinks to choose from back at rehab. I'm not in the market for more."

She put a hand on Max's shoulder. "It's not bad that you care about Simon. I'm really glad that you do. Kids pick up on that kind of thing instantly— they know if you really care or if you're just going through the motions. I'm sorry you didn't have a Violet or a Grannie Annie in your life, but don't you think it's amazing that you get to be that for someone like Simon?"

She could almost watch his defenses rise up to cover the deep truth of those words. "I'm no Violet Sharpton." He sloughed off her comments, hitting the remote button that opened his car doors. "Don't blow this up into more than it is."

"You're more like her than you know, Max. I'd have never believed this at first, but I think you're just what Simon needs—most of the time." She still wasn't convinced Max wouldn't go a step too far one of these days. Then again, how many times had Violet done something that made everyone groan? And still, there wasn't a single person in Gordon Falls who didn't love her or want her around when things got tough. Max had that gift. There was something deeply enthralling about how he hurled himself into the world. He just hadn't tempered it with much wisdom yet. With time, would he?

She couldn't answer that question, and that jolted a small wave of panic through her chest. Max Jones was exciting and energizing to be with, but that unfocused energy also made him dangerous. As Max's smile made her heart flutter a bit, Heather knew the danger wasn't just for Simon. He ran his hand over hers for just a second before he got into his car, and the tingle told Heather just how much she'd begun to fall for Max Jones. *Oh, Lord, guard my heart. This is either going to be wonderful or awful, and I'm scared already.*

Chapter Eleven

Max was spending a quiet Wednesday night trying not to think of Heather Browning, previewing a new Adventure Access video and going over some of JJ's files from the cabin-rental business when his cell phone went off. He flipped it over and pushed the speakerphone button when he saw Simon Williams's name on the screen. "Hey, Simon, what's up?"

"I hate him!"

"Slow down there, big guy—hate who?"

"Who do you think?" Simon's voice was a tsunami of teenage anger. "I hate him like I've never hated anything."

Max picked up the phone and switched off the speaker function. "You mean your dad?"

"He treats me like I'm a total baby. It's so embarrassing."

"You're fifteen. Your parents are supposed to be

embarrassing when you're fifteen." Max had the disturbing thought that JJ would be fainting to hear him offer such advice. Dad and he had been about as compatible as snowballs and campfires in high school.

"I thought you'd understand!"

The accusation stung. He did understand. He was supposed to be the one guy who *could* understand. "No, I get it. I do. Where are you?"

"I'm in your driveway. By your car."

It was almost nine o'clock at night on a Wednesday. "You're here? For crying out loud, why didn't you just come to the door?"

"I couldn't figure out which cabin was yours." Max could believe it. Simon sounded mixed-up enough to not know his left from his right.

"Look for the ramp. It's the one right in front of you as you leave the parking lot. Number Four. I'll throw the porch light on for you." Max ended the call, tossed the phone into his lap and wheeled toward the door. He snapped on the light and pulled the door open to find a red-eyed, scowling Simon.

"Hi."

Max pushed back to give Simon room to come in. "Hi yourself. How'd you get here?"

"I walked." He managed a sour smile. "Well, you know. It's not that far and mostly downhill."

"I can't believe I'm playing the grown-up here, but do your folks know where you are?"

"I hope they don't. They're at school, at parent-teacher conferences." His eyes narrowed to angry slits. "They got me a sitter."

"A what?"

"Someone to stay with me so they could both go to the conferences. I'm fifteen years old and they hired a babysitter. Can you believe it?"

Max didn't know what to think, except that said sitter, whoever he or she was, was likely calling the high school in hysterical fits right about now. He was going to have to handle this very carefully. "How'd you sneak out?"

"Candace was so engrossed on her phone it wasn't hard. She's not too bright, so I left the door open just to drop a hint."

Max nodded toward the kitchen. "Want a soda while we talk this though?"

"Sure."

Max chose his words carefully as he reached into the fridge. "I agree the sitter was lame, but she and your parents are probably freaking out right about now, don't you think?"

Simon softened a bit. "I s'pose."

"So." Max slid a soda across the kitchen table to the boy. "How about I call Heather and she can go find your mom and dad at school and talk them down off the ledge? Otherwise, I expect we'll be hearing police sirens roaming through town in ten minutes. She can hold them off for a bit while you and I figure out your next step. Sound like a plan you can live with?"

"Okay."

Max punched in the listing for Heather's cell. She picked up after half a ring, her voice tight with panic. "Max? Do you—"

He didn't let her endure another second of worry. "It's okay," he cut in. "Simon is here. He's safe, just mad." He thought Simon had some good justification, but now wasn't the time to get into that. "He just showed up at my door about five minutes ago."

"Oh, thank goodness." He could hear shouting in the background as Heather turned her voice from the phone to address what had to be Mr. and Mrs. Williams. "He's safe—we know where he is." A woman began to cry.

"You've got to buy me twenty minutes, okay? Simon and I need to talk this through."

Mr. Williams's voice bellowed, "Where is he?" over Heather's line.

"Max, I—" she cautioned.

"The kid needs someone to listen to him, Heather. And that won't be Mom and Dad right now. You know that. Just do what you can and I'll call you back as soon as the air is clear." He ended the call before she could say anything else. If she succeeded, he might stand a chance of keeping Simon from boiling over. If she failed, Simon's parents would be breaking down his door in five minutes anyway.

Max wheeled over to the table, flipping the pop tab on his own soda with what he hoped looked like calm. "I bought you as much time as I could, Simon, but it isn't much. Why don't you tell me what's been going on?"

"They treat me like I'm five. I could be driving next year, but they don't even let me alone yet. Worst of all, this time they hired a *girl from school* to come stay with me. A junior, even. This'll be all over school by second period tomorrow. You know it will." Simon let his head drop into one hand. "I'll never live this down."

Max took a swig of his soda to buy himself time to craft a calm answer. What Simon described would have been social homicide back in his day, and he didn't think that much had changed about high school. "Was she cute?"

Simon looked up. "You're kidding me."

"Just looking for the silver lining here. Was she cute? Did she know she was essentially babysitting?" Max hoped Simon's parents were smart enough to call it something else, but it wasn't likely.

"She was okay. She made a half-baked attempt at getting math tutoring from me, but she found her phone a lot more interesting, if you know what I mean."

"Tutoring, huh? Simon, there might be a way to salvage this. A freshman guy tutoring a junior girl is a pretty good gig. Your mom and dad would have been smarter to work this out with you ahead of time, but there's a chance we can keep this from disaster. What did you say her name was?"

"Candace Norden."

"Do you know her cell number?"

Simon rolled his eyes. "Do I look like the kind of guy who can get a junior cheerleader's phone number?"

"Then we'd better pull Heather in on this. Okay if I call Ms. Browning again?"

"Do I have to talk to my parents?"

Max sighed. "Not yet if you don't want to. But if we want Candace's cooperation on this, we ought to let her know you slipped out on her and that you're okay. If we can get everyone to agree on the story that you were tutoring her, I think we can save this. Although it could mean you might actually have to tutor her, so it helps that she's cute and a cheer-leader, right?"

Simon shot Max a "you don't really think this is gonna work?" look, but he nodded.

Heather again picked up right away. Max gave a quick account of the situation and his plan to res-cue Simon's social standing. Heather agreed it was worth a shot and got Candace's cell-phone number from Simon's parents, who seemed to have calmed down a little but not enough. At least they weren't breaking down his door. "Try to give me thirty min-utes, Heather. See if you can get them to agree to work with Simon instead of stuffing bad plans down his throat."

As soon as he hung up with Heather, Max dialed Candace. He put on his most charming tone of voice, the one that had broken hearts back in the day. "Hey, is this Candace?"

"Who are you? Do you know where Simon Williams is?" She sounded upset, and Max took that as a good thing.

"This is Max Jones. Simon's right here, Candace. Things have gone a little haywire tonight, and I'm trying to sort it all out. Do you have a car?"

"Yeah."

"Simon is at my house. I live at the Gordon Cottages down by the river. Number Four. Can you meet Simon and me here so I can explain? It's okay—his parents know he's here now and you can call Ms. Browning at the school if you want her to confirm everything."

"No, it's okay. You're the other guy in a wheelchair, right? I know who you are. Give me ten minutes. Simon's okay and everything, right?"

"He's fine. And make it five if you can." Max hung up the phone and looked at Simon. "You know, I remember a time when *you* were 'the other guy in a wheelchair.' Now it's me. And she's worried about you. This might actually work out."

"I don't see how it can."

"It's simple. We charm Candace into agreeing

that she was there tonight for math tutoring, which will probably involve you helping her score at least a B on her next test. Then we tackle the hard part of enlightening your folks that there might be less socially destructive ways of handling this stuff. Then you agree not to go AWOL like that again. It was understandable but totally counterproductive. You do know what—"

"I know what *counterproductive* means," Simon cut in. "But I was so mad. How could they possibly think that was okay?"

"They're parents. High school freaks parents out. And your parents? Well, they seem especially... freakable."

"You've got that right."

Max offered a smile. "Go hit the bathroom and wash your face. There's a girl coming over soon."

Two long hours later, Heather stood on Max's porch, waving goodbye to the Williams family as they headed home after a difficult evening for everyone. She turned her eyes to Max, who looked equally exhausted. "What a night. At least they were speaking to each other when they left."

"I feel for that kid. He's got a long battle to become his own person." Max looked up at her. "Do you think they understood him at all tonight?"

She leaned against one of the porch railings. "I want to think they did. Her more than him, I think.

Usually it's the moms who can't ease up on the supervision, but it seems to be Brian who's the hoverer in that family."

"Firefighters tend to have a wide protective streak in them. JJ babied me a bit at first after my accident, and she's not even my mom." Max rolled his shoulders, looking weary from the intense conversation they'd all just had. "I'd forgotten how brutal high school can be. I sure hope this works. Simon is right—if this got out, he'd never live it down. I can't believe they don't feel like they can leave him alone. He's fifteen and pretty capable."

"Maybe after tonight they'll start figuring out how to give him some freedom. But he's going to have to keep from pulling another disappearing act." She walked over to Max. "Thank you for saving the day."

Max rubbed his neck. "I'm not sure I saved anything yet."

"You persuaded Candace to help out. You got them talking to each other about what Simon needs. That's huge."

"Yeah, but you're the one who kept them from shouting at each other. And me. Well, mostly."

Some shouting had definitely taken place. Brian Williams had harbored suspicions that Max had put Simon up to his escape, but Heather had managed to convince him that wasn't true. "You're a good man, Max Jones. Do you know that?"

"Don't kid yourself."

"I think God knew what He was doing when He put you in Simon's life. He cut off my access to the other mentor because He knew you were the man who would understand and bond with Simon."

Max flung his hands wide. "I'm the only other guy in a chair for miles. There's no grand design here, Heather."

Had life shaken his faith that far? She'd thought she'd seen more than this dismissal back at Mort Wingate's funeral. "You can't really mean that. You can't tell me you don't believe God spared you, or that He spared you for no good reason."

Max swiveled away from her. "Most days I don't think God spared me much of anything. I hear all the stuff JJ says to me, but I can't really swallow God loving me enough to snap my spine."

She'd never heard such dark words from him. "So you've no faith? None at all? Even after something like tonight happens?" She hadn't realized until tonight how much she was yearning to take things further with Max. He'd been a dangerous prospect before, but the way he'd talked to her after the funeral told her there was so much more running under the flashy exterior. Without faith—or a hope of faith—she couldn't begin to risk it.

He must have heard the catch in her voice, for he turned back to face her. "I don't know if it's gone or jumbled or what. I know I could have—maybe *should* have—died when I fell. I know my accident brought Alex and JJ together, and I see all the good that's come out of it. I'm glad I can help Simon. But…"

"But what?"

Such a shadow of pain crossed Max's eyes that Heather felt it like a slash to her chest. "But I'm still broken."

Heather came down onto her knees in front of him. "Oh, Max, we're all broken. You, me, Simon, the Williamses—all of us."

"I know there's a part of you that thinks I'm the same as any other man, Heather, but it's a load of—"

She grabbed his hand and shook it. "You're *not* the same as any other man. No other man could have done what you did tonight with Simon. Could you have done what you did tonight, what you've done all month, before you fell?"

He pulled back away from her. "I wouldn't have *had* to do any of this if I hadn't fallen. Can't you see that? I'm not you. I'm still angry. I'm angry at God for letting any of it happen at all, even if JJ got Alex out of it. 'Cause you know what? I'm selfish enough to wish it all hadn't happened. I hate that it happened. I don't want to make the best of it. I want to walk. There. I said it. Are you happy?"

Heather sank down to sit on the porch, wounded. JJ was right: Max still really was "too much of a mess to mess with." She wanted to shout *No!* in answer to his question, but the word couldn't find its way beyond the massive lump in her throat.

Her silence seemed to break his anger, and he covered his face with one hand. "I'm…sorry. That wasn't fair. I didn't mean to hurt you." He slammed his hand on the porch rail next to him. "Hurting you is the absolute last thing I want to do."

"Faith doesn't deny pain exists. Pain—and your pain is huge and real—means that you need faith just to keep going."

"How do you do it?" There was a seeking desperation in his voice.

"I don't. I can't. I just beg God to do it in me, for me, because I'm still a mess on the inside. It just shows less with me. Only you can still see it. I know you can."

The Max she'd first met had looked as if he could do anything. The Max who stared back at her now looked as if faith was far out of his reach. If she knew anything, she knew that wasn't true. "I'm not as strong as you think I am, Max."

"Sure you are." His voice held a sad resignation. "You're amazing."

Heather didn't know where the courage to do so came from, but she grabbed the footrest of his chair and pulled it toward her. "I mean I'm not strong enough to do this without faith. I've got mine, but I need to know you've got yours." He kept his hands on the wheels at first, not letting her pull, but then slowly let go.

"I don't know where mine went." All his famous bravado left him, and Heather's heart cracked open.

She pulled him closer. "So let's go look for it. You and me. Because I don't think God dropped you, Max Jones. I think He caught you just in time."

He looked at her for a long, soft moment. She could see him fighting the shadows of doubt, feel the man he was wrestle with the man he could be. She was shaking inside, deeply scared, but she would not allow herself to back away or break his gaze.

He brought one hand to her face, trailing the curve of her cheek with the same tenderness he had at the ice rink. She felt the same swirling sensation, her hands clutching the front rails of his chair to keep her balance. Without a word, he moved to hold her face in both hands, looking down at her with a powerful air of wonder. The whole world held its breath as she rose up to meet his kiss.

Max was light and careful, as if the kiss were stolen rather than freely given. Yet the way the kiss made her feel was anything but light; it was deep and daring in a way Heather had not thought she could experience. She'd tried to tell herself Max was troubled and cocky and careless, but her heart refused to accept that outer shell as truth. The Max she could see underneath was also strong and seeking and full of courage. God could do amazing things with Max if he would only let Him back in all the places he'd shut Him out.

She sent her hands sliding up his arms as he wrapped one hand around her waist. The kiss was perfection, tender, passionate, exquisitely slow. She let one hand wander into his hair, marveling at the touch of it.

His sigh rumbled low and smooth like his car engine. "Whoa," he said, pulling her hand from his hair. "You'd better not do that."

She smiled. "I've wanted to touch your hair for days."

He took her hands and placed them on his chair's armrests. "Ms. Browning—" he cleared his throat in a mock-professional manner "—every male of the species has a weak spot. A place where if you touch them just the right way, they can't even think straight."

Her grin widened.

"Now you know mine. Be careful with such powerful knowledge."

She flushed at the sparkle in his eyes. "Does that mean I have to tell you mine?"

Now his eyes fairly smoldered. "I think I already know." With that, he reached out and feathered her cheek again, producing such a head-spinning sensation that Heather had to fight to keep her eyes open. "I promise not to use it against you."

With a slippery, falling feeling, Heather realized she wished he would.

Chapter Twelve

Mrs. Williams hadn't gotten any more sleep than Heather had, and she looked it. There had been a message waiting on Heather's voice mail, time-stamped just after dawn, asking for a meeting. "Just you and me. I thought we ought to talk," Mrs. Williams had said in a soft and weary voice.

"How are things with Simon?" Heather gestured toward the guest chair in her office.

"Difficult." She chose the word with care.

"If teenagers are anything, it's difficult." Heather came around to pull up the second guest chair so that they could sit side by side with no formal desk between them. "If it makes you feel any better, I thought last night ended well, considering the circumstances. I've seen much, much worse over much, much less."

"Simon's never done anything like that, ever." Hurt coated her words.

"He's finding his way in a new, wider world. They make lots of mistakes at this age. Did he talk to you this morning?"

Mrs. Williams winced. "Barely."

"Sometimes 'barely' is all you get with boys his age. It's a rough ride, but if you can just keep the communication flowing, I know you'll get through it. Simon is an amazing young man. He copes with things other kids his age couldn't handle, and he's making good choices." Given last night's escapades, she felt compelled to add, "Mostly." She put a hand on Mrs. Williams's arm. "What can I do to help you?"

The woman looked as if she had rehearsed these questions since dawn. "What kind of man is Max Jones, really? And how much influence does he have over my Simon?"

Heather sighed. "I know you have reservations about Mr. Jones. He certainly has his share of faults. But you ought to know that I think Max was a large part of why last night wasn't a disaster."

Mrs. Williams ran one hand through her hair. "I don't think Brian sees it that way."

"I wouldn't expect him to. Simon has been trying on a lot of new independence since he met Max, and I'm sure that hasn't been comfortable for you and your husband. Only—" Heather leaned in "—I think it's really important for someone Simon's age to have another adult—one that isn't Mom or Dad—

to turn to. Simon needs someone who understands what life is like in a wheelchair, and I can't help him with that. None of the teachers here can."

Mrs. Williams's expression softened a bit. Heather's heart twisted for the woman—she couldn't even begin to imagine the strain of parenting someone like Simon. She'd seen what her personal trauma—minor and fleeting compared to Simon's—had done to her own parents.

"You're doing an outstanding job with Simon—please believe that. Last night only proves he's a normal teenager, not that you are faulty parents."

She managed a weak smile. "Thank you."

"So, hopefully, you can see why I'm really grateful Simon has Max. Try to see it as a good thing that Simon went to Max last night. Try to be grateful Max helped your son when Simon was angry enough to make a choice we all might be regretting this morning."

Mrs. Williams bit her lip. "Simon idolizes Max. He'd do whatever Max told him to do. I'm sure you can see how unnerving that is for us. Max seems so—" she looked for a polite term for what Heather knew she was thinking "—wild. The car, the hair, the risky sports…" She finally gave up and blurted out, "We don't want Simon to end up like that."

Heather folded her hands. It was going to take a little work to keep her personal opinion out of this professional conversation. "Max hasn't let his limitations stop him from doing anything he sets his mind to. These are good things. They're things I know you want Simon to learn. Sure, he's a bit… outrageous, but that's because he thinks for himself and isn't afraid to be different. That's the most important value Simon can learn, and I don't think it will mean Simon will become someone who doesn't hold the values you've taught him. In short, Mrs. Williams, I think you can trust Max Jones. He's earned my trust and Simon's, and if you give him a chance, I believe he'll earn yours."

"Well…" She stood up to leave, still not looking especially convinced. In fact, her expression told Heather she was sure trusting Max Jones would lead to a Simon with ripped jeans, spiked hair and an adaptive motorcycle—if such a thing even existed.

Heather stood up, as well. "May I suggest something?"

"Yes."

"Try not to let last night limit the time Simon and Max spend together in the next week or so. Simon's going to need to talk through what happened, what he felt and the choices everyone made. The more he understands his own feelings, the better he'll be able to tell you what he needs and wants. A little more communication will go a long way to keeping stunts like last night from happening again." She touched Mrs. Williams's elbow and offered her a warm smile. "Although he *is* a teenage boy. I can guarantee you it won't all be smooth sailing. I have high hopes for Simon, and I think you should, too. Even with last night's drama."

"I'm glad you think so." She turned to leave. The slump of her shoulders left Heather wondering if she'd been remotely successful in comforting this poor parent.

"Please keep in touch. Any questions at all, I'm available. And I'll let you know if I see anything that concerns me."

"Thank you." With a small nod, Mrs. Williams left the administrative offices. Heather would have liked it better if she hadn't clutched her handbag so tightly as she walked down the hall, but she couldn't really fault Mrs. Williams. Parenting in high school was a harrowing business—mostly because being in high school was a harrowing business. She knew that better than anyone.

Margot Thomas stood in her doorway and waved Heather inside. "I heard."

Heather put a hand to her forehead as she walked into Margot's office. "Rough stuff all around. I think everyone's okay, though."

Margot sat down on her desk. "Did you see this coming?"

Collapsing into Margot's guest chair, Heather replied, "Yes and no. I figured Simon would eventually do something to brandish his independence, but not this soon. To be honest, I'm just a bit thankful it wasn't something on school grounds, where Simon's parents could project the blame on us. Everyone could have behaved better, but there's a part of me that can't blame Simon for pushing back against a babysitter at his age."

"Did he really get all the way from his house to Jones's cottages by himself?"

"Evidently it's not that far and all downhill." Heather smirked. "Who knew?" She felt her smirk dissolve into a weary sigh. "I'm just so glad Max was there for him."

Margot leaned back in her chair. "Heather, I want you to understand that I'm speaking as your friend, not your principal, when I ask, just what is your relationship with Max Jones?"

Heather held the woman's eyes for a moment, unsure of her own answer.

"I couldn't help but notice that your admiration of him seemed to go beyond the professional."

Heather gripped the chair arms. "I…"

Margot raised a hand "Hang on—I'm not saying that's bad. Neither of you have done anything wrong. I'm just saying we might need to take a little extra care here. You just made some pretty big promises on Jones's behalf to Mrs. Williams, and I just want to make sure you spoke as a counselor, not a young woman who's spent a lot of time with a very charismatic man." The older woman's words were cautious, but her eyes held a mother's twinkle.

Margot had stopped just short of setting Heather up on several dates over the past two years.

"I do trust Max. I do think he's good for Simon. And I do think Mrs. Williams can trust him."

Margot took her glasses off. "Why?"

"I thought you said you heard what I said. I think Max is making the most of his life despite what's happened to him. I think he represents all kinds of possibilities to Simon right now, and that's a good thing. And okay, yes, I think Simon's parents need to learn to loosen up a bit, and Max can show Simon how to help that happen. In ways that don't involve sneaking out and rolling across town."

Margot didn't reply, but her eyes narrowed to say she didn't entirely agree.

"What?"

"I'm not so sure that was the counselor talking. A counselor might be pushing for moderation, for small steps of independence that can build trust and bringing in someone that would be a slam dunk for parental approval. That does not describe Max Jones."

"No, he's not the obvious choice, but Simon needs someone daring."

Margot leaned in. "Does Simon? Or do you?"

JJ poked her head through a life ring labeled Jones River Sports. "Max Jones saves the day. Never thought I'd hear that." Max and JJ were storing some of the warm-season gear away for the winter after he got home from work Thursday night.

Max fastened the straps on another life jacket and tossed it into the wire bin at the back of his storage shed. "Where'd you hear such nonsense, anyway?"

"Brian Williams."

Max spun around. "Brian Williams said that?"

"Well," JJ amended, "Brian Williams explained a situation that could be interpreted as you saving the day. I don't think he shared the view. He doesn't like you very much, actually. Some part of him still thinks you put Simon up to his escape."

"I didn't." Max deposited the last life jacket from JJ and shut the bin's lid. "But I can't say I wouldn't have done the same in his place. A babysitter? At his age?"

JJ started bringing oars in off the dock. "Brian never leaves Simon alone. Never has, from what I gather. It's a bit over-the-top, but can you blame him?"

Max grabbed the oars out of JJ's hands. "As a matter of fact, I can. They're smothering him. Next time he's going to have to do something twice as dramatic to pull free, and who knows what'll happen?"

JJ upended a bucket and sat down on it. "What really happened last night?"

"You just told me you knew the whole story." Max slid the oars into a barrel.

"I mean after Simon left. There's something you aren't telling me."

Max looked JJ square in the eye. "None of your business."

"It *is* my business if it has to do with you and my friend. Heather looked just like you do now." She wiped her hands off on a nearby towel and tightened her ponytail elastic. "Look, I know I said I wasn't for you two getting into it, but come on—something is going on. It's obvious."

JJ was military. Trying to keep secrets from her was about as effective as the huge green flood doors that sat at the end of town—they worked for a while but eventually things seeped through the cracks. "I like her. And if last night's kiss was any indication, I think she likes me. I asked her out to dinner tomorrow night. So, yes, something is going on."

JJ's eyes popped at his blatant disclosure of facts. "You kissed her?"

"Actually, I think she kissed me. But it turned entirely mutual very quickly. And close your mouth, sis. It's not like I'm twelve."

"Heather kissed you? First?" Her shock was rather annoying.

Max headed for the door. "See, this is why I didn't want to tell you." An oar landed in the doorway to block his path. "Cut that out. You're not getting any more details. I'll try to behave myself, if that's what you're worried about." He angled to face her. "Believe it or not, I'd actually like to do right by the woman this time. If that's okay by you."

JJ looked satisfyingly aghast. "Yeah, I suppose."

"Why don't you just try to be happy for me? I may have just cleaned up my act, after all. Stranger things have happened."

JJ sat back against the wall, squinting at him as if he was a puzzle she couldn't quite solve. "I was just thinking the same thing." She pulled the blocking oar toward her, her expression softening. "She could be really good for you, Max. And you might just be good for her. Don't mess this one up. Not this one."

"No," Max said, holding her gaze. "Not this one."

Chapter Thirteen

Max could not remember the last time he was this nervous. An actual date. Was he ready for this? Did he even know how to do this? *You used to be fantastic at this,* he told his reflection in the rearview mirror as he pulled up to Heather's apartment Friday night. *This is just fantastic Max on wheels, remember?*

It wasn't true. No matter how he tried to talk himself out of it, Heather wasn't just any girl. Something in him had come completely unwound when he'd kissed her, something he wasn't quite ready to let loose. *Imagine that—me not ready to let loose on something.* He ran his hands through his hair one last time. *Get a grip, Jones. You used to be so much smoother than this.*

He pulled up Heather's number on his cell phone and called.

"Hi." She picked up right away, a bit breathless.

Her anticipation zinged through him. How long had it been since he'd felt the wonderful buzz of a first date? Startled, Max realized he'd kissed Heather before he'd started dating her. That was a first. Taking the time to get to know a woman before he dated her wasn't the usual Max Jones style.

"I'd come to your door, but that might set us back another twenty minutes." He tried to make a joke of it, but the fact that Heather's apartment was a second-story walk-up stung just a little bit too much.

"I'll be down in a jiffy." Max craned his neck up to see her waving out her front window.

Max clicked his phone off and then checked again to see that the passenger seat was set in right. He had no intention of making Heather ride in the back tonight.

She pulled open the door to her building and paused in the light of the entrance. Max wondered if her breath hitched the way his just did. For years JJ had lectured him on the difference between "a hot girl" and "a beautiful woman"—and it had just sunk in. Heather was beautiful. Not just in the way she filled out the peach-colored dress she wore or the way her hair swung about her shoulders, but in who she was and the light in her eyes. The pain in her eyes, too. She was so much braver than she gave herself credit for, so much stronger than she realized. And this amazing woman was about to get into his car and have dinner with him. Him, the guy in a chair. Tonight, just about anything seemed possible.

It bugged him that he couldn't open the door for her. She didn't seem to mind, easing herself into the passenger seat and smiling at him. "You said to dress up a bit—is this okay?" She tucked a strand of hair behind her ear.

Okay didn't even begin to describe how she looked. "You look incredible." Every ounce of cool aloofness left his voice, and he found he didn't care.

She flushed, and Max felt a glow settle under his ribs. "You look pretty good yourself. You should look beyond your T-shirt collection more often." She fastened her seat belt. "Where are we going?"

Max had chosen the restaurant with care. "The Black Swan."

Her eyes went wide. "The Black Swan? Can you get in there?" As if she realized the discomfort of that question, she backpedaled. "Of course you can get in there, right?"

It was too late. The dent in Max's confidence had already been made. Well, they were both new at this—no one could expect a completely smooth ride tonight. "I called and checked. Besides, they legally have to have a way for me to enter. Although I did get the feeling they don't do a lot of wheel traffic." In fact, the maître d', Jeremy, had been effusively confident—something Max had learned to take as a warning sign. He'd almost switched restaurants after the phone conversation, but The Black Swan was the nicest restaurant in town and he wanted to do tonight right.

He pulled into the handicapped spot right out front. "I'm probably the only person in Gordon Falls who never had to complain about how hard it is to get a parking spot on Tyler Street on a Friday night."

She laughed, but a tiny bit too much.

"They've got a ramp that fits over the front stair. Why don't you go in and let the maître d' know we're here while I get out of the car?"

He was pleased she didn't seem fazed by the request. "Sure thing."

She slipped out of the car, and with a mild rush Max noted her scent in the wake. Something flowery with a little bit of vanilla. It made him want to get her close to him and take deep breaths until his head spun. *Easy, boy. Take your time with this one.*

By the time he'd come out of the car, he saw Heather looking frazzled while a pair of busboys fumbled with a metal ramp. "I don't think they've used this before," she told him with a cringe.

"Really?" Max forced the frustration from his voice, trying to sound as if this sort of thing happened every day—which, unfortunately, it did. "Whatever gave you that idea?" Thankfully, the model in question was one he had seen before. He rolled up and pointed to the end at the bottom of the stair. "It goes the other way, boys. The lip goes on top. Slip the pins in before you put it back down and everything will be just fine." He raised one eyebrow to Heather. "We ought to hint at a free dessert for this."

A small crowd of people had gathered on the sidewalk to see what the fuss was about. Heather bit her lip and clutched her handbag. "It's fine," he assured her, touching her elbow. "Just minor logistics."

She flashed him a too-wide smile. "Sure." She was trying so hard.

Normally, Max enjoyed making an entrance. He was jazzed to be able to show the good people of Gordon Falls that a guy on wheels could take a lady out for a nice evening. Fine dining wasn't always his thing—no one could call him a "foodie" unless Dellio's burgers counted as cuisine—but he knew his way around an upscale table like The Black Swan. As long as the maître d' didn't—

"Good evening, ma'am."

—direct all his comments toward Heather. Right here, right now, was the absolute worst part about being in a chair. The people who looked down on him. Not just physically—he'd long since stopped letting sight lines bother him—but figuratively. As if the loss of leg function implied loss of brain function.

"Jeremy," Max cut in perhaps more sharply than was necessary, "I believe we have reservations under Jones for seven o'clock? You and I talked on the phone this afternoon?"

Jeremy had the good sense to look sheepish. "Of course."

"You might want to have a talk with those two working the ramp out front. They don't seem to have any idea what they're doing, and I'd like to exit the place in one piece when we're done."

"Certainly." The guy shot a questioning look at Heather, as if to say, *Is he for real?* Or perhaps it was *I had no idea.* The evening would go better if he gave poor Jeremy the benefit of the doubt.

That generosity lasted until Jeremy showed them to a table way off to the side of the restaurant. With no view of the river and entirely too near the kitchen. He tapped Jeremy's elbow and gestured for him to bend down—knowing that it only made Jeremy more uncomfortable. "I distinctly remember us discussing a table overlooking the river. This is kind of a special occasion. Can we do a little better?" He kept his words kind but put enough bite in them to let Jeremy know he meant business.

Jeremy's furtive glance around the restaurant soured Max's stomach. He held the maître d's gaze and then nodded toward an empty table for two beside the big beautiful windows now framing a dramatic fall sunset.

"Max," Heather whispered, "it's okay."

"No," Max insisted. "It's not." He looked straight at Jeremy. "Do we have a problem?"

"No, sir. I don't believe we do. Give me just a minute."

If Jeremy had just kept to his word and cleared a path to the table Max had requested, they would not have had to make the scene of asking two people to stand momentarily and move their chairs aside. Max thought about clueing Jeremy in to Karl's free-coffee policy, but he decided against it. Heather was turning four shades of pink next to him, nearly squinting her eyes shut as the server pulled out her chair and settled her into the lovely table overlooking the river.

"Did you have to do that?" She cringed when the server left.

"Actually, I did. It's always hard to wake people up to their misconceptions the first time, but I want to be able to take you here anytime I want and be able to request a table like any other patron." He softened his voice. "This is my world, Heather. Very few things are easy. And I get a lot of stares."

When she looked down, he reached across the table to take her hand. "But staring at you is very easy. You look fantastic. Really. Can we forget about Monsieur Idiot back there and have a nice dinner?"

He could literally see her choose to be brave. Could other people see her swallow that desire to hide, or was it just him? He usually loved his role as "human icebreaker," nearly relished the rolling wake-up call his life had become, but knowing the attention made her uncomfortable tainted the experience for him.

Well, what do you know? Max Jones finally cares about someone else ahead of himself. Talk about your wake-up calls.

The man's eyes could steal the air from the room. When Max looked at her like that, Heather fairly tingled. He was this force of energy, this freight train of courage and conviction that never seemed to let anything stop him. She was ready to believe that Max was moving past the bitter anger of his initial response to his injuries. He would be—in many ways already was—a conqueror who tackled one obstacle after another. A man to admire.

A man who was showing off tonight. If Max Jones loved to do anything, it was show off. Normally, she didn't care much for such theatrics, but the fact that he was showing off for her? It peeled off her reluctance one charming smirk at a time.

"Oh, hey, in all the tussle I almost forgot." He reached into his pocket and pulled out a ridiculously small gift bag. She recognized the pink and yellow from Jeannie Owen's candy store, and smiled at the vision of Max Jones shopping in all that sugarcoated fluff. Jeannie must have had a field day with Max.

"What's this?"

"Open it."

Heather tugged on the tissue until a small, fat marzipan flamingo and a handful of other chocolates emerged. The gift was just like Max, touching and a little bit outrageous at the same time. "A candy flamingo?"

"I saw it in her window yesterday and I couldn't resist. I remembered the one from your desk the day we met." Those last words took on a glowing tone she couldn't ignore. "You thought I was nothing but trouble that day."

Heather held his eyes a moment. "I was wrong."

His smile was smoldering. "Oh, I'm still trouble."

"You're a fine man. You're an insp—"

His hand shot up. "Please don't say *inspiration*. I hate it when people call me an inspiration. I'm just making the best of the hand I was dealt."

Why did he always sell himself short on something genuine like that when he was so quick to boast about things that didn't really matter? "I admire you, and you can't stop me." She'd meant it to come out lightly, but the truth of her growing feelings shone through instead.

Now it was his turn to stare into her eyes. "It's not your admiration I'm looking for." His eyes glanced away for a second, and he licked his lips. Was he nervous? The realization made her heart flip-flop. "I'm just a man, Heather. Like every other guy out there, only with a pair of wheels."

She took his hand. His fingers were roughened from all the time they spent pushing his wheels, but they were warm and she could feel all the power he gained from them. "You are not like every other guy out there." She spoke slowly, sincerely. "And I'm glad."

He interlaced his fingers with hers, his thumb running distractingly down the side of her hand. "Well, I hope you're as hungry as you are happy, because I plan for us to eat well tonight."

He relaxed into the evening as the meal progressed, the sharp comments falling off into something that felt much more like deep conversation. She loved watching the hard shell peel off him, enjoyed asking questions that coaxed the more tenderhearted man she'd glimpsed on his porch that night to come back out. He spent so much energy coping, pushing and blazing trails in the world that it was as if he'd forgotten how to just be. The Max on parade was flashy and fun, but the offstage version was a quieter, doubting, near poet of a guy who was quickly stealing her heart.

A jazz combo had started up earlier on the restaurant's outdoor patio, the velvety tones perfectly matching the still-warm indigo evening. "Can you really take me dancing?" she asked as she finished off the last of her chocolate cake dessert.

"Ooh, the lady remembers my offer."

"We did have a rather unforgettable first meeting."

Max put his napkin on the table and signaled the server. "We've had a few memorable moments since then. So you want to dance, do you?"

She felt her face flush. "I'm not really sure how… you…do that."

His eyes grew downright mischievous. "You worried you're going to have to lead?"

Suddenly, there was no adventure she wanted more than to dance with Max, however he managed to do it. "I don't think you know how to follow anyone, Max Jones."

He paid the bill and nodded toward the door. "We're going to have to go down by the river, but I think you can still hear the band."

She gave him a suspicious look. "Are you trying to get me alone?"

"That's a grand idea, but mostly I just need a little more space than your average prom date."

Thankfully, the pair of busboys had left the ramp in its correct position, so Max rolled easily out of the restaurant—after two more people had to shift out of his way. Once they were out, he turned the corner and said with a dashing grin, "Hop on."

"What?"

"You ever ride a grocery cart in the supermarket?"

"Sure, but…"

He tapped his knees. "Same thing, only different."

Heather didn't think it was anything like any grocery cart ride she'd ever taken. "Can you…hold me?"

"I'm not made of glass, darlin', and holding you is the whole idea. I'll be just fine."

Feeling a bit ridiculous, Heather climbed gingerly onto Max's lap. "Keep your hands in your lap and lean to one side a bit so I can see where we're going." She followed his instructions, and Max coasted the downhill slope of the street like a carnival ride, going slow enough to make her feel safe but just fast enough to tug a small squeal from her as he turned onto the short stretch of concrete that spread under the patio of The Black Swan. Music and light spilled out into the night, creating their own little dance floor.

The music flowed into a lazy samba, and Max hoisted her out of his chair as if she weighed nothing at all. Keeping one hand on her elbow, he spun her to face him, then took each of her hands in his. "I pull— you push." Sure enough, she began to move with Max, pushing apart and pulling together like dancing partners. He spun her, and she laughed. "See? You're a natural."

Emboldened, Heather lifted up her arm, and Max deftly spun underneath it, catching her waist as he went by and sending her twirling in the opposite direction. Back and forth, spinning in small arcs and big dramatic circles, she enjoyed the dance more than she'd ever have imagined. Max knew how to pull fun from life like no other man she'd met. All the awkwardness of the earlier hours melted away in the lure of his eyes and the strength of his hands.

"Put your foot here," he coached, nodding to one of his footrests. She tucked her toe in next to his as he pulled one of her hands to his shoulder. She raised herself up on tiptoe beside Max on his footrest, the other foot extended out behind her in a playful pirouette. Max spun her around, making her feel like the tiny ballerina on her childhood music box, twirling under the stars in a dazzling finish as the music ended.

Heather curled, slowly and effortlessly, into Max's lap as if it was the most natural place in all the world to be. He tilted his chin up toward her; the colored lights of the patio above them played across his face and shoulders, lighting the unchecked affection in his eyes. She moved closer, watching her hair tumble around his features until it curtained the moment when her lips met his.

The kiss was sweet and urgent at the same time. It wasn't a hungry, devouring kind of kiss, but, while it was slow and soft, it was still driven by a need to be close and closer still. Awe. That was what she felt in Max's kiss. The starstruck wonder that they'd ever met at all. It coupled with her own astonishment that he met such a deep need in her; they matched beyond what either of them ever expected.

She felt him smile and heard a low, delightful laugh rumble from him as she settled down to sit on his knees. Max ran his fingers through her hair, sending tingles out through her fingertips. "That," he said, his eyes bright as the starlight on the river current behind them, "was officially wonderful."

She couldn't help but laugh herself. "You are a very good dancer."

"Surprised you, did I?"

She leaned in again. "In a million ways."

Chapter Fourteen

If anyone had told Max he'd spend a Sunday night making a complete idiot out of himself with a Ping-Pong ball and a straw in front of a tableful of teenagers, he'd have laughed in their faces. The youth-group brand of fun was never his thing, even when he was the age to be in one. None of which explained how much he was enjoying himself tonight. This riotous version of "air hockey" had him laughing and puffing so hard he was starting to feel dizzy. With a conspiratorial look to Simon, Max sent the Ping-Pong ball the boy's way and Simon shot it into the makeshift goal on the opposite site of the table. Victory hoots shot up from "Team Si-Max," lording their conquest over a gangly sophomore and his uncle, the town banker.

"We advance to the finals after dinner!" Simon pumped his fists into the air. Max gave him a high five, enjoying the boy's enthusiasm. It was clear the boy felt less stress here than at school.

"I'm too old for this," complained a grandfatherly type Max recognized as George Bradens, the retired fire chief and Clark's father.

"Aw, c'mon, Chief—you used to be full of hot air," another man Max vaguely knew from the firehouse kidded George. Max had fun watching the two tease each other. His own dad was always so serious and task oriented—Max could have never invited his father to something so raucous as Friends Night. Max found it a pleasant surprise to know that, at least at Gordon Falls Community Church, "spiritual" didn't always have to mean "serious."

"Hey," Simon pointed out, "Ms. Browning is here."

Sure enough, Heather sat down at a dinner table with a gaggle of high school girls. "She didn't mention she was coming," he replied, trying to keep the warmth of her tender kiss from creeping into his voice. He hadn't seen her since that night, and the memory flashed through him as he watched her laugh at something. She was really getting to him.

"She shows up for dinner a lot. She's like an adviser or something."

During dinner, Max tried to keep up a conversation with Simon and meet his friends while at the same time he could feel Heather in the room with him. He would sense her gaze and look up from spaghetti or chocolate pudding to find her eyes across the room. It was as if the world were moving on two different levels—one with Heather and one with everyone else. He couldn't decide if the sensation was unnerving or exhilarating. Maybe even both—a whole new thrill for this consummate thrill-seeker.

He was elated when Team Si-Max took first place in the air-ball finals, winning an absurd trophy fashioned from tinfoil-covered paper cups. "Our champions!" Heather beamed, giving Simon a quick hug and Max one that lasted just a bit longer. Max was starting to find the scent in her hair downright addictive. From the flush in her cheeks as she stepped away, he was starting to have the same effect on her. "So, how are you enjoying Friends Night?"

"It's not at all what I expected," Max admitted.

Simon launched a superior look at Max. "*Told you* it'd be fun."

"You did. And you were right. Try not to lord it over me, okay?"

"I dunno." Simon's face lit up in the smirk that was quickly stealing Max's affections. "That'd be hard." He looked at Heather. "I need something to drink after all that huffing. Want anything?"

"I'm okay. I'll supervise Max while you're gone—just so you don't worry." Max had always found *sparkling* such an overdone description for a woman's eyes, but the word sure fit tonight.

"Yeah," Simon said as he headed off toward a

tub of ice filled with bottles of root beer. "He can't be trusted."

"Funny." Heather sighed as Simon wheeled off to join some friends. "I told Mrs. Williams just the opposite Thursday morning."

Max's mood lost some of its joviality. "Convinced I was behind Simon's escape, was she?"

"I think she's just trying to figure out who this new Simon is and whether or not the changes she's seeing are a good thing. Don't fault her for her suspicion. I've got files of stories of teens led down wrong paths by the very adults who were supposed to be helping them."

Suddenly, it was crucial that he know. "Do *you* think I'm helping Simon?"

"I do, and that's exactly what I told her. I think the fact that Simon felt he could come to you kept him from making a far worse decision Wednesday night." She tucked her hands into her pockets, and Max knew why. The urge to reach out and touch her was so strong, but this wasn't the time or the place. Max Jones erring on the side of discretion. It was a wonder the world didn't tilt in alarm. "Yes." She sighed the word in a way that spread a cheesy but wonderful glow in Max's chest. "You are helping Simon more than probably either of us will ever know. Will you cringe if I call you an answer to a prayer?"

Max had been called a lot of things in his day, but never that. "Yeah, I will. But go ahead."

Heather could barely contain the bubbly joy she felt watching Max and Simon say good-night as the evening's victors. There was no formal reason for Heather to be there tonight. As a youth-group adviser, she was welcome at any of the Sunday night youth-group events, and she'd wanted to watch Max discover how much fun church could be. Her heart was in a dangerous place with Max: if things were going to move forward, she wanted to know faith was becoming a part of his life. The way he looked tonight—laughing and cracking jokes and meeting people—that was as much a gift as his exquisite kiss. *Am I ready to trust him with my heart? Has Max healed enough to be slow and careful with it? Or will I be hurt again?*

"Hey there."

Heather turned to find Melba Bradens. "Hi. Your father-in-law sure had a good time tonight."

Melba's sigh reminded Heather it had barely been two weeks since Mort's funeral. "It's good to be silly after all that other stuff."

"How are you feeling?" Heather touched Melba's arm. "Is it still really hard?"

"Yes." Melba blinked back a few tears. "And no." She smiled. "I wanted you to hear it from me."

"Hear what?"

Melba's hand slid to her stomach. "I'm pregnant. A little girl. In March."

Heather wrapped Melba in a huge hug. "Oh, that's wonderful. Really wonderful." She pushed the woman to arm's length. "You don't even show. I mean, you do—you look wonderful. Did—" she was almost afraid to ask "—did your father know?"

Now a tear slid down Melba's face. "We told him." She laughed and swiped the tear away. "Actually, I think we had to tell him about twelve times, but I'm positive it sunk in."

"That's so sweet. What did he say?"

"He asked if we could call her Maria after my mom. He actually laughed and said he was glad it was a girl because he'd feel bad asking us to give anyone a name like Mort." She sniffled. "I would have, you know? Well, okay, maybe as a middle name, but I would have."

Heather squeezed Melba's hand. "So it'll be Maria Bradens?"

Another tear escaped to slide down Melba's cheek, and Heather felt her own eyes brim over with the bittersweet balance of it all. "Clark gets to choose the middle name, and he hasn't done that yet, but yes." She managed a damp laugh. "He made a joke about Morticia the other day, though, so I know he's working on it."

Heather leaned in. "So, how many pairs of baby booties have you knit?"

Melba winced. "Six. It was the only thing I could do until I could tell everyone. I've knit dozens of baby booties before, but in a way I feel like I've been waiting my whole life to knit *my* baby's booties. That's kind of sick when you think about it, isn't it?"

"Not at all. Congratulations. I'm so happy for you and Clark." One of the reasons Heather wanted to learn to knit from Melba was so that someday she would be able to do exactly what Melba was doing. It had always stung her that she'd never found the time to let Grannie Annie teach her to knit before the wonderful old woman had passed on. How many pairs of socks had Grannie Annie knit for her as her leg was healing? Families were where healing was born. How life went on. Heather hoped that when God gave her a family of her own, she'd glow just as much as the woman smiling in front of her.

"So what about you and Max Jones? Don't think I didn't notice the way he looks at you. And let's just say your dinner at The Black Swan didn't go unnoticed."

Some days it seemed as if nothing in Gordon Falls was ever private. Not to mention how impossible it was to blend in beside Max. Heather wasn't quite sure she was ready to be that public about Max, even to a friend like Melba. "He's doing wonderfully with Simon."

Melba leaned back against the wall and crossed her arms over her chest. "That's not what I asked."

Heather felt her face heat up. "Well, maybe there's something there, but…"

"Oh, there's something there all right." Melba's eyes were kind behind the teasing.

Heather simply pushed out a breath and shrugged her shoulders. "I don't really know yet. Parts of him are so amazing. But he's wild and loud."

"Well, you know what they say about opposites." Melba cocked her head to one side, offering a smile. "Maybe you'll be perfect for each other." She looked into the room, where Max was telling some rousing and evidently funny tale to an audience of teens. "The kids love him. That's always a good sign, right?"

"Not if it's because he's just a great big kid himself." Mr. Williams had said something to that effect after lambasting Max for aiding and abetting Simon's escape.

Melba gave a small hum. "Maybe you should get your eyes checked, because that is most certainly a man. A handsome man who can't seem to stop staring at you."

"I just need to be more…sure…than I am now. It's going to take time, and Max doesn't strike me as the patient type."

"So give it some time. I have a feeling Mr. Hot Wheels might just surprise you."

Heather nodded. She was certain Max would surprise her. She just couldn't be sure if the surprise would be a happy one.

Chapter Fifteen

Two days later, Max found himself in an Iowa college library. Such academic surroundings were not his home territory. An internet search was about the furthest he'd go in the name of research, but he'd uncovered a story of a World War II wounded aristocrat funding a nature-path renovation that would accommodate a wheelchair, and he thought it would make a nice bit of info to add to an event AA was planning in another Iowa city. The scarcity of available materials meant actually going to a library to do it old-school—microfiche readers and old files of yellowing newspapers. At first it seemed like a pain, but it was getting too cold to go out in the *Sea Legs* and Max had decided he needed the three-hour drive to think over everything that had happened lately.

"May I help you?" the librarian asked.

"I need newspaper files from 1980 to 1984 on the

Baker trail-system renovation. Your website said those aren't electronic yet, right?"

"No…sir, they're still on microfiche. Our electronic archives only start in 2000." Max found it amusing that she seemed to have to think about whether to call someone dressed like him "sir."

"Can I get to the readers and the files in my chair?" Max pictured a musty file room down several flights of stairs.

"You can access the readers fine, but I'll have to bring the hard-copy files up to you one year at a time."

It sounded as if he was going to be there for a couple of hours. "That'll work for me. Lead on."

The librarian removed the chair from in front of one of the ancient-looking microfiche reading machines, gave him a few slips to fill out and within fifteen minutes Max was trudging his way through endless images, feeling like one of Heather's high school students working on a boring research paper. Academic research was definitely not how he liked to spend his time.

By the third reel, Max needed a break. He wheeled up to the reference desk and put in an order for the files of hard-copy issues he'd managed to identify as likely sources for the information he needed, then asked for directions to the nearest decent cup of coffee.

The diner half a block down was not only

accessible, it had free internet access. Max flipped open his laptop for a little twenty-first-century coffee break, deciding that not all small Iowa towns were boring and backward.

Come to think of it, Heather had said she was from Iowa, hadn't she? Would an internet search bring up any high school pictures of her? Had the town made a big deal when she'd graduated despite such a traumatic injury? Normally, Max wasn't in the habit of cyber-sleuthing women of interest, but the query seemed the perfect way to recharge his history-numbed brain cells. Counting backward, he guessed her high school graduation at somewhere around 2004, typed that and her name into his search engine, and started in on his very good coffee.

He found four photos of the small graduating class—there couldn't have been more than fifty students—and a pair of articles on "inspiring seniors." Heather looked young and fresh-faced, a cheerful but wobbly smile under her mortarboard cap. She had the beginnings of the beautiful woman she was now, but a shy and cautious nature came roaring through in the way she posed for pictures. In fact, he saw more of Simon in those photographs than the Heather he'd come to know.

The Heather he'd come to care about. A lot.

He clicked a few associated links, ending up at two articles covering her accident and the resulting burns. Another article covered the driver's charges—the ones that had so angered Heather's father. Max could see where Heather's father's fury came from: the article was clearly written to cast the boy as a victim of his youthful indiscretion. There wasn't a single mention in that article of Heather's injuries and the resulting medical consequences.

It was the next set of links that dropped his jaw. They were from a few years later—her senior year in college, as far as he could tell. They were engagement announcements. Heather had been engaged.

She'd never mentioned it, and he'd have thought something that significant would have come up in the conversation by now. Who was this Mike Pembrose, this all-American farmboy-looking guy who had captured Heather's heart in college? And, more importantly, what had broken them up? He began clicking on links about Pembrose, curious and surprised at the jealousy rising in his gut.

Pembrose was a medical student. "Dedicated," one hometown paper announcement declared, "to the treatment of the diabetes that has afflicted him since childhood." That felt significant, although Max couldn't say why.

Two more links led to bits of information: one was an announcement of Pembrose joining a medical practice last year in Des Moines, his name mentioned on a fund-raising committee. The second, a post in a forum for diabetics, gave him the most telling detail of all. The comment thread was about when a man should tell his girlfriend he was diabetic. Pembrose—at least it sure looked as if it was Pembrose—wrote a long post about how challenging the issue was for some couples. "As involved as my disease was, my girlfriend knew about it, but we never really discussed it. I never tested in front of her. I kept my insulin out of sight. I never talked about the complications. That was a dumb thing to do, but I think I knew somewhere inside that she couldn't handle it. I learned I was right. She ended up breaking off the engagement—my future marriage yet another victim of the Big D."

That didn't sound like Heather. Then again, did he really know her that well? It was a few years ago, but could someone's basic nature really change? And given the nature of their conversations, why hadn't this come up? Why hide that she'd been engaged before?

Granted, this was Pembrose's side of the story—and at least the guy had the decency not to call the lady out by name—but could it be anyone other than Heather? Luke Sullivan's words about women came back to him: *They only think they can handle it. Then everyone finds out how ugly it can get.*

She's different, his heart argued with a force Max hadn't expected. *No, she's not different,* his head countered. *When you let her in far enough to see all of what it's like, it'll be over. Sullivan said it. Pem-*

brose said it. Could he even hope to have enough of a sense of things to call them wrong?

Talk to her about it. Alex had taught him the virtues of going straight to the source when a problem arose. Only he knew what would happen if he did. She'd swear by her loyalty now. She'd say all those sweet and hopeful things that turned his jaded defenses inside out. She'd convince him. He'd believe it because she'd believe it. And then, like Mike Pembrose, he'd be too far in when the bottom fell out. Reality never had to play fair—wasn't he walking... *rolling* proof of that?

Max slammed his laptop shut and stared out the diner window at the charming little town. It looked like someplace Heather would have grown up, all quaint and friendly and rural. Then the corner of his eye caught the three people from the counter staring at him. They averted their eyes the minute he met their gazes—no smiles, no friendly hellos, just the embarrassment of having been caught gawking. For a handful of moments Max considered getting in his car and heading west instead of back east, of just ditching the whole "have a real life" dream and embracing his life as an oddity drawing stares.

You can't do this alone. The infuriating truth was that Max needed other people to survive: doctors, aides, money, an accessible place to live. He couldn't pretend not to need JJ; for all his bravado, he wasn't ready to be all alone.

Max stared at his now-cold coffee. *I don't know what to do.* He was surprised to find the thought feeling closer to a prayer. Alex always said he went to God with his problems—and Alex was the best, most creative problem solver Max knew. Heather, JJ and many of the other nice people at Gordon Falls Community Church had said the same. None of that made him feel better. *I don't know who to believe,* he admitted, still staring into the fragrant brown liquid. *I can't believe God, Heather, Sullivan, Pembrose and Alex all at the same time. I'll have to choose.*

"Oh, no!" Heather dropped the file she was holding as Simon Williams rolled into the administrative suite with blood all down one side of his face. "Simon, what on earth happened?"

"Three guesses," Simon said with a sneer, his voice dark and sharp. He spun his chair toward the nurse's office as the door behind him filled with the algebra teacher, a hefty man who was currently wrestling a fuming Jason Kikowitz into the office by one elbow.

"No," Heather said in disgust more to herself than to anyone else. "I'd hoped we were past this." She shot up a quick, silent prayer for wisdom, squelching her own rising temper.

"Mr. Kikowitz" came Margot's equally displeased

voice. "What a disappointment to find you in my office again."

Heather stood up, momentarily stumped as to whether to head left toward the nurse's office or right toward the principal's. Simon won, and she walked to the left. "Simon, are you all right?"

"Fine!" Simon barked, slamming the nurse's office door shut behind him. Clearly, he didn't want questions right now. At least not from her.

"I don't know what Jason said to him in Study Hall," the teacher said, wiping his hands off with a tissue from the secretary's counter, "but suddenly there was a whole herd of them shouting. When Jason tried to tip Simon's chair over, Simon turned on him and rammed him so hard Jason fell over. It went downhill from there."

"Stupid baby raked my shin open with his baby carriage, that's what!" Jason pointed to his bloody shin. "I've got a game on Friday and this hurts like—"

"Enough!" Margot cut in before Jason's language went south. "What did you say to Simon to start this?"

"Candace Norden told me she got hired to be Simon's babysitter."

Heather slumped against the wall, her eyes closed in a wave of regret.

Jason went on. "Little twerp made fun of my algebra grade—"

"Your *failing* algebra grade," the teacher cut in, earning a "don't make this worse" look from Margot.

"So I called him a baby who needs a babysitter. Then he called me a thug."

Heather winced. "Thug" had been Max's term of choice for Jason.

"You can imagine how things went from there," the teacher concluded.

Margot steepled her fingers. "Jason, this isn't the first time. This isn't even the first time with Simon."

"He hit me!" Kikowitz actually sounded surprised. "And not just with his chair—the little nerd actually tried to punch me."

Heather's stomach began to tie in knots. This was not the kind of confidence she was looking to foster in Simon. *Please, Lord, do something!*

"I'll find out soon enough if that's true, but let's keep this conversation about you. I warned you if there was another incident, I'd have to suspend you. I don't make empty threats, Mr. Kikowitz. You're suspended for two days beginning immediately. And that includes Friday's game."

"But we're playing Bradleton on Friday!"

"It might have been helpful to remember that before you baited Simon Williams into a fight. Straighten up, Jason. Any more suspensions and you risk your graduation." As Kikowitz took a breath to launch an argument, Margot stood up and called out past Heather to the school secretary, "Please call Mrs. Kikowitz and inform her Jason is to leave immediately and why." She pulled some forms out of her desk and handed them to Jason. "I know you drive to school, so I suggest you go straight home. These must be signed by both your parents before you can return on Monday. What you do next could decide your whole year, Jason. I'd take some time to think about that if I were you."

Jason stood and kicked back his chair. He stared daggers into Heather's eyes as he stomped past. "Gonna defend your little handicap project, are you?"

"No," Heather said, her voice a lot calmer than she felt. "I think he did that all on his own, thanks." She'd never wanted to call a student the slew of names that flew through her head right now. How did someone so young get so mean? For all his saber rattling, Jason wouldn't last two weeks facing all the challenges Simon or Max endured. Someone needed to take that boy down a peg before his arrogance ruined his future.

And Candace. How could Candace go and betray Simon after promising Max she wouldn't? Max's brilliant solution was falling apart right in front of her and there didn't seem to be anything she could do to stop it. There were only three periods left in the day, but that was more than enough time for word to spread about Simon's "babysitter." This was a disaster.

The nurse's office door opened, and Simon emerged, a series of bandages on one cheek and a few more on his right hand. His shirt had a rip in one shoulder and blood on the collar. He looked as dark and angry as Heather had ever seen him.

"Simon." Margot's tone held the cool, soft edge of a principal about to do something she hated. "In my office, please."

Heather made to follow him, but Margot put her hand out. "No. I think you'd better sit this one out."

Heather left the office, walked calmly to the faculty washroom, locked herself in the last stall and cried.

Chapter Sixteen

Max wasn't in the mood to go home after his discovery at the library, so he stopped off at the Adventure Access offices. He'd banged around for an hour, pretending to work, but was just about to call it a day when he looked up to see Heather coming in the office door. Headquarters was at least twenty minutes west of Gordon Falls and, from the looks of it, she had fought tears the entire drive. All his agitation over what he'd learned pushed itself aside as he grabbed the box of tissues off a credenza and met her as she sank onto the couch that served as AA's meager waiting room.

Alex and AA's equipment guy, Doc, were out setting up a trade show, so this afternoon the office was staffed by just Max and Brenda, a bright young amputee with wide eyes and outstanding computer skills who handled the phones and the other administrative tasks. At four employees, AA wasn't big enough to have individual offices, placing workplace privacy at a premium.

Brenda grabbed her crutches while she sent Max a look of understanding. "Hey, I was just craving a latte, so I'm going to the corner, okay?" Max shot her a grateful smile before returning his attention to Heather.

"What's happened? Why'd you come all the way out here?" He nodded toward Brenda's desk. "We've got phones."

His attempt at humor fell far short of the mark. She almost didn't need to ask "Has Simon called you?"

"No." He checked his watch, the early hour doubling his worry. "School's still in session and he's not supposed to call then, which makes me wonder why you're here. Heather, what's happened?"

Her eyes turned as hard as he'd ever seen them. "Jason Kikowitz is what happened." She pulled a tissue from the box Max held out to her. "Well, he and Candace."

Max felt bile climb the back of his throat. "She didn't."

"That or Jason got it out of her somehow. Does it matter? Kikowitz let the whole story loose in Study Hall, and it escalated into name-calling and punch-throwing. On both sides."

Max wanted to hit something. Or someone. Hard.

"That overgrown creep of a... Wait, did you say both sides?"

"Yes. Simon and Kikowitz got in a fight. Simon deliberately rammed him with his chair and then threw punches at Kikowitz. You can imagine what result that got."

"Simon fought back?" Max shook his head. "Good for him."

"No," Heather nearly shouted. "Not good—it's bad. Simon can't hope to match a brute like Kikowitz in a fight. Besides, it's not the way to solve something like this. All it got Simon was a week of detentions and a split lip." She glared at Max. "I can't believe you'd think Simon fighting is good." Her eyes narrowed. "And maybe that's half the problem right there."

Max ran his hands down his face. "You'd rather Simon just lie there and take the kind of grief Jason Kikowitz dishes out?" Heather's resulting expression told him she expected just that. "I thought the whole point here was to give Simon the confidence any other kid his age would have. Any other kid his age would have fought back. Or at least tried to. Sure, I would have loved it if the whole business with Candace never came out, but I knew there was a chance it would fall apart. And I knew that if it did, it would be up to Simon to decide how to handle it. Didn't you?"

She pushed up off the couch, pacing the room.

"No. I had more faith in you than to coach Simon to stand up for himself like that."

Max swiveled to face her. "Whoa, there—listen to what you just said. It's not bad that Simon stood up for himself and it's not on *me* that he did. I did not coach him to pick fights with Kikowitz. I'm the guy who persuaded Candace to keep it quiet, remember?"

"It didn't work, did it?"

"It was a long shot and I always knew it. You want someone to blame? Blame Simon's parents for hiring a sitter in the first place." Max threw his hands up in disgust. "They're behaving like he's five years old. Even you have to see there's no medical reason he can't be on his own for a few hours."

She knew he was right about that; he could see it in her eyes. "It's not my job to tell someone how to parent their child."

That sounded like too convenient an out, and he was already mad at Heather. "You're supposed to have Simon's well-being in mind, his growth into a—" Max searched for a sufficiently clinical term "—successful young adult. I'm telling you his parents are standing in the way of that. Brian Williams handed Simon to Kikowitz on a silver platter the way I see it. For Simon to lie there and take the ridicule and abuse without defending himself would have made it ten times worse."

Heather stood there, hands on her hips. It burned

him that she willfully stood over him—she'd never pulled that kind of tactic before. "That is way out of line, Max, even for you."

"How can you stand there and tell me Simon is at fault?" He pushed back away from her, needing distance and finding it infuriating to have to crane up to look her in the eye. "I don't see how you can think it's okay to give him detention when Kikowitz was picking fights with him. It's like there's no self-defense clause in high school."

She followed him. "There *is* no self-defense clause in high school. Zero tolerance means exactly that. Hitting back is the same as hitting. I don't know how your world works, but I don't have the luxury of shades of gray. Simon's just as guilty of fighting in school as Kikowitz."

"So the guy can wind up and do it again tomorrow and Simon's supposed to just duck?" Whether it was a logical conclusion or not, Max's gut was boiling as if Simon were being thrown to the wolves. And he was coming to care too much for the little guy to just stand by and watch him get eaten. "How fair is that?"

"Jason Kikowitz is expelled for two days and barred from playing football this weekend—but only because it's his third offense." Heather threw away the first tissue and grabbed a second, now pacing around the greeting area. "I don't know what the punishment is for Simon because Principal Thomas *excluded* me from the meeting."

Ouch. That began to explain why Heather was here instead of at work. He'd have stomped out of the office at a shutout like that, too. Even though it was a dangerous question, he ventured a "Why?"

She turned to bore into him with fierce eyes. "Seems I may have lost my professional distance on this one."

The hurt in her eyes dug sharply into his chest. The size of her heart was what made Heather so wonderful and so impossible—she couldn't invest halfway. She couldn't be careful with her affections. Only she had done just that with Pembrose, hadn't she? He wanted to grill her about it but knew this was far from the time for that conversation. When had the stakes in all this become so personal? What was he supposed to do now? He tried to form a response but came up empty.

His silence seemed to deflate her. She sank back onto the couch. "I've failed Simon in the worst possible way. My job was to help him avoid things like this and now look." Her words were soft and wounded.

Heather's despair cut through his anger. As hard as she was being on him, she was clearly blaming herself, too. "I don't see it that way."

She narrowed her eyes. "And how do you see it?"

"You think this could have been avoided, but it

couldn't. Simon's gonna get picked on no matter what you do." The office phone rang, and he let it go to voice mail. "If you think that by some marvel of programming or counseling you can protect Simon from jerks, you're dreaming. The jerks are out there. They always have been and that won't change anytime soon." He wanted to move closer, drawn by the failure that seemed to drag her shoulders down so hard, but his own hurt demanded he keep a distance. "Thinking Simon can be protected from them makes you just like Mr. and Mrs. Williams, trying to keep Simon under glass." He knew that brand of suffocation and was happy to help Simon push back against it. "Look, I am sorry Simon got punished, but I can't see my way to being sorry he stood up for himself the way he did."

Her hands fell open on her lap. "How can you say that?"

"Even you have to know how guys like Kikowitz work. He's trolling for weakness. As soon as Simon shows even a bit of strength, he'll go looking elsewhere. It's not a perfect solution, I agree, but I don't think this is the full-out failure that you're making it."

"Oh, and his right hook to Jason Kikowitz is proof of my effectiveness?" She cocked her head at him, puzzled hurt all over her face. "I can't believe you're okay with this."

Max swallowed. She'd been deeply hurt and she'd

driven twenty minutes to him for comfort. Even he wasn't too much of a jerk to not realize that ought to count for something. "I'm not okay with it. I hate that it happened. You're upset. Simon disappointed you." Feeling Mike Pembrose's comments banging against the back of his brain, he forced himself to add, "He's lucky you care so much about him."

"I do care about Simon. Margot's right—I have lost professional distance. I just can't shut it off, you know? He's so special." She looked right into his eyes and Max felt as if she could see far too much there. "He's got all these special people in his life now."

How was it this could be the same Heather who hadn't been strong enough to stand by her fiancé? Had the war zone of working in a high school strengthened her? Could he risk his heart on that? *My world would eat you alive,* he thought. If she could get so worked up about Simon, if she could walk away from Mike Pembrose just because he was a diabetic, how could he ever think she could handle what life slung at him every day? She needed to be made of much tougher stuff if they were ever going to make it, and she just wasn't the tough-stuff kind.

If Brenda hadn't appeared in the door, he might have dared to ask her about that history. As it was, Heather said a flustered goodbye and hurried out.

Max couldn't decide if he wanted to thank Brenda or curse her.

He settled for texting Simon.

Heather didn't go home. She couldn't face the walls of her empty apartment, not with the way her feelings were in their current state of jumbled mess. *Did I fail Simon, Lord? Is there something I need to learn from this?* She drove to the riverbank, wanting the solace of the water and knowing Max wasn't there right now. The little dock off Max's cabins seemed a good place to sort things out.

October was such a beautiful time in Gordon Falls. The trees were spectacular, God's exquisite palette splashed across a clear blue sky. The air was just nippy enough to feel clean and crisp, not yet cold enough to bite. Now, looking out over the flowing river, it was easy to think the world was moving along as God intended—not as humans had hopelessly muddied it up.

"It's my favorite place to think, too." Heather turned to see JJ, a bucket of cleaning supplies in her arms and a curious smile on her face. "Shouldn't you be in school, young lady?"

Heather moved over on the bench, patting the space next to her. "I got asked to leave. Actually, no, that's not true. I got shut out of a meeting and I stomped off. Not exactly exemplary behavior."

"Not like you at all, either." JJ sat down. "What on earth happened?"

Heather slumped lower on the bench. "A fight broke out at school. Simon—Brian Williams's son, the one Max is helping—and Jason Kikowitz."

"Kikowitz beat up on Simon?" JJ cringed. "Didn't he try something earlier this year? He laid into Simon again?" She shook her head, her long blond ponytail swinging as she sighed. "Why some kids can be so mean..." She met Heather's eyes. "Is Simon okay?"

Heather ran her hands through her hair. "It depends on who you ask. I think it's terrible that Simon tried to fight back, but your brother thinks it's a good thing Simon is standing up for himself."

"Sounds like my Max all right." JJ pulled her knees up and hugged them. "Bullies like Kikowitz make me so angry. Max did his share of terrorizing in high school—he ought to know better."

The memory of Simon's wounded eyes brought the lump back to Heather's throat. "I was so sure Max's idea was going to work."

"What idea?"

Heather related Simon's escapade, Max's solution, Candace's promise and the subsequent betrayal. She left out the part about Max's heartbreaking admission and the kiss that still took her breath away. She was falling for Max, hard. "He's doing amazing things for Simon, JJ. He has such a heart, if only..."

"If only he'd stop shouting so loud?" JJ finished for her, a wistful smile on her face. "I know." She looked out over the water. "You know, I'd have never said this at first, but Max is a better man on wheels than he was when he could walk. It's changed him. I think he'll continue changing." She returned her gaze to Heather. "With the right person beside him. Has he figured out how much the two of you have fallen for each other yet? Or do you think you'll have to hit him over the head?"

Heather felt her jaw go slack. "You know?"

JJ laughed softly. "I'm his big sister. And your eyes light up when you talk about him." She nudged Heather. "Even when you're complaining about him. That's a contradiction I'm very familiar with."

"At first, I was so sure he and Simon would end up a disaster—no offense." Heather put her hands to her cheeks, certain she was blushing like a teenager. "And then I thought he was exactly what Simon needed. And now…I have no idea."

"Well, he's not done yet. Mr. Hot Wheels is a bumpy ride—I don't have to tell you that. But his heart is in the right place on this one, and I think Simon has a few things to teach Max."

"I think so, too." Heather recalled the energy in Max's eyes when he talked about Simon—the boy brought out something extraordinary in Max. It was close to the unforgettable glow she'd seen in his eyes when he'd looked at her that night on his porch.

There was so much tenderness in that man that the world never saw. Could she bring out something extraordinary in Max? She knew he was bringing new and marvelous things out in her.

"I think you're really good for him, Heather. I admit, I was nervous at first—Max was a veteran heartbreaker before the accident—but I think God's up to something here."

"Oh, I…"

"He was really touched by the knitting ladies, you know. I'm sure he never admitted it, but he talked about them for half an hour when I saw him the other day. Alex and I have been trying to drag him to church again since the funeral, but *you* made it happen." JJ pulled in a deep breath. "Can you imagine what God could do with a guy like Max? The people he could reach? The lives he could change?"

She'd had the same thought herself. Max never did anything halfway—if his faith ignited, it would be spectacular. "He told me he's still angry at God for dropping him."

A sister's heartbreak filled JJ's eyes. "I know. What did you say when he told you that?"

"I told him I believed God caught him just in time."

Affection replaced the heartbreak in JJ's features. "What did my little brother say to that?"

Heather took a deep breath. "He kissed me. Actually, I think I may have even kissed him first."

JJ blinked back tears, something Heather hadn't seen this tough warrior of a woman do very often. "I was wrong, Heather. I think you're good for Max. Really good. Don't give up on him when he makes a mess of things, okay? He needs you."

I think I need him, Heather thought. *But he needs You most of all, Lord. You'll have to shout loud to get through to Max Jones.*

Chapter Seventeen

Max's wheels skidded on the firehouse floor as he zoomed in one of the open bay doors. The older guy everyone called Yorky looked up from the supplies he was shelving. "Hi, Max. JJ's in the kitchen."

Max knew the way, but his path ended up being blocked by the tightly packed tables in the dining room. After a conversation with Simon an hour ago, Max was angry enough to knock over every table in the county, but that wouldn't solve anything. Frustrated and stalled, he resorted to yelling "JJ" until her head popped out of the pass-through window from the firehouse kitchen.

She'd either talked to Heather or Brian, because she already knew. Her expression said that loud and clear. Fine. He wasn't in the mood to recount the gruesome facts anyhow. She took her time coming out of the kitchen, wiping her hands instead of looking him in the eye. Without a word, she moved a series of chairs so they could sit at the farthest dining room table. "You want a soda?"

As if that would help. "No," he snapped. "I do not want a root beer to make it all better." He liked the stuff, and the firehouse was always in full supply of Gordon Falls's official beverage, but he wasn't even remotely in the mood.

"I'm sorry about what happened to Simon." After a second, she added, "Aren't you supposed to be in Iowa today?"

"I was." He didn't want to offer any further explanation than that.

JJ frowned. "I know you've invested a lot in that kid. I'm really sorry he got a week of detentions. Doesn't seem fair, does it?"

Max ran his hands down his face. "According to Heather, it's all equal as far as the school's concerned. Kikowitz's mean left hook is just as punishable as Simon's weak attempt to fight back." He looked up at JJ. "Am I wrong for being glad Simon tried to stand up for himself? If it was me, I'd have slugged the guy, too."

JJ offered a melancholy smile. "You did, back in school. Twice, if I remember right."

Max laughed darkly. "I beat up Noah Morton for leaving you at the homecoming dance, didn't I?"

"Not your best moment, but you meant well."

"He's going to keep baiting Simon—I know he is. The kid's a predator, and he's picked out Simon as the weakest of the herd. Someone needs to teach that bully a lesson."

"That someone is *not you.* The last thing Simon needs is you deciding to show Jason that a guy in a chair can throw a decent punch."

"Do you know how much I want to?" Max planted his elbows on the table, hands fisting at the thought of what Jason had done to Simon for no reason other than pure meanness. "If I saw him across the street right now, I could—"

JJ put her hand on Max's arm. "But you won't. Max, Simon looks up to you. What you do now is going to teach Simon how to deal with the world. Look, you've made some progress with Brian—he told me so just yesterday. You're helping Simon. Don't blow it all to pieces over someone like Jason Kikowitz."

Max rested his forehead on his upright fists. "I'm just so…mad. We work so hard to give people an equal shot and guys like Kikowitz can wipe it all away in ten minutes." He'd always wondered when his passion for Adventure Access would rise to the level of Alex Cushman's, but he hadn't counted on it happening out of sheer vengeance. He doubted this was the kind of motivation Alex would condone.

"Go take the boat out, go shoot hoops with the guys here until you've burned it off, but *burn it off.* Don't show Simon the wrong way to handle this."

Max simply groaned. He really wasn't in the mood for a big-sister lecture.

"We just had a training session, so there's a bunch of the younger guys out back. Go shoot hoops." As if to drive the big-sister thing home, she stood up and planted a kiss on the top of his head. "It'll feel good."

He knew what would feel *terrific* right now, and it wasn't the condoned plan of behavior, that was for sure. Anger boiled up in him like a furnace fire, heating his thoughts and shredding his patience. This thing with Simon and Kikowitz touched on so many parts of his life, he couldn't seem to escape it. He couldn't outthink it, couldn't solve it, couldn't appease it; he could only endure it. While he had a lot of physical endurance, his emotional endurance had pretty much run dry in the months since he'd fallen off that cliff.

"Hot Wheels!" Jesse Sykes waved to him from under the basketball hoop that stood at the little concrete yard in the back of the firehouse. "Good. I need somebody I can beat." He bounced the basketball straight at Max.

Max caught it in one hand, aimed and sent it through the hoop. "You mean you need a beating to take you down a notch." The sound of the ball clanging through the chain net was satisfying. They started a rousing game of one-on-one, which eventually became two-on-two as some of the other guys came out to join. Without making a big deal out of it, these guys always found a way to make Max feel as if he fit in. It just made him ache harder for Simon to have the same experience.

He missed two shots in a row because his thoughts were tangled around Simon's plight, losing the game for his team. Jesse reached into a bin and tossed Max a towel. "What's up with you?" Jesse asked, wiping the sweat from his own brow.

At first Max hesitated—talking about it would just make it all surge back up. Only these guys knew Brian Williams as one of them. They knew Simon, and many of them had taken a shine to him like Max had. Maybe they could help the boy feel as if he wasn't so alone. "It's the thing with Simon Williams."

"Oh, man," said Wally Foreman, collapsing on a bench that sat at the edge of the concrete. "Heard about that."

"I had Kikowitz's older brother in my class when I was in high school," another guy shared with a grimace. "Big and mean runs in the family, if you know what I mean."

"I've never seen Williams so mad," Jesse said. "That kid means everything to him."

"I feel for Simon," Wally offered. "Hard to live something like that down, you know? Kid's gonna hear *babysitter* called after him in the hallways for years." A little geeky himself, Wally's eyes went hard and narrow. "I hated high school."

Jesse leaned in. "I hate to say it, and I'd never tell Brian how to parent his son, but I was glad to hear that Simon stood up for himself this time. That kid needs to strike back and strike hard if he's ever going to be able to hold his head up at that school. Guys like Kikowitz feed on this stuff unless you shut them up."

The churning in Max's gut was growing by the minute. "I can't tell you how much I want to string that kid up by his expensive sneakers and show him he's not as tough as he thinks he is."

Wally raised one eyebrow. "So why don't we?"

Jesse stilled. "What are you saying?"

"I'm saying we should show Kikowitz that the Gordon Falls Volunteer Fire Department looks after its own. You mess with Williams's kid, you mess with us. I'm not saying we should hurt the guy, just give him reason to think twice before he gets into it with Simon again."

"Let Simon know we've got his back." Jesse nodded.

Stop this, a little voice in the back of Max's mind whispered. It was far too easy to ignore it. "I don't think Brian would go for it." Some part of him knew the weakness of that objection.

"Who says Brian has to know?" Wally grinned. "Probably better if he doesn't, actually."

"I'm in," Jesse said. "I'd happily put Kikowitz in his place. A little community service, if you ask me."

This is wrong, the little voice began to shout. It sounded way too much like Heather. Well, all Heather's ideas and spiffy activities hadn't helped Simon one bit, had they? Bullies only spoke one language, and Max had been fluent at his age. He'd know just how to pick on Kikowitz's weak spots. He'd tell the guys how best to frighten Kikowitz but stop them before they went too far. Simon would know there were more people on his side. "Appealing as it sounds, we can't hurt him. This has to be a warning, not a payback. And I can't really be involved."

The three other guys looked at him.

"But I can drive."

Heather rested her head in her hands the next morning and tried not to cry. The only grace was that Jason Kikowitz's father had railed at her on the phone rather than coming in to personally convey his outrage at what had happened last night.

"I agree this is an awful development, Mr. Kikowitz, but as it didn't take place on school property, I'm not sure what I can do." A group of three young men—and there was little doubt in her mind who at least one of them was, even though she couldn't quite yet figure out how, since no one had yet mentioned a wheelchair—had cornered Jason in the parking lot of Dellio's diner last night and pushed him around, shouting threats should he try anything else against Simon Williams.

"Jason tells me the hoodlums that roughed him up got into a dark car with flames painted on the sides," Mr. Kikowitz growled into the phone. "He said you'd know who owned that car, Ms. Browning. Do you?"

The "yes" of her reply felt like thorns in her throat, sharp and wounding.

"What are you going to do? I demand you do something about this!"

That was just it—this problem was so enormous and so painful she couldn't even think of how to respond. It was as if Max had handpicked the worst way to betray her trust, the most painful act to shred everything that had grown between them since that night on the porch where she'd told him he wasn't broken. She was wrong. Max was broken, and he'd now broken everything else within reach.

"Are you listening to me?" Mr. Kikowitz yelled. "Do I have to take my son's victimization up with the police?"

Victimization. While what happened to Jason was wrong in every way, did his father really see his son as a victim? Did he have no sense of how Jason had begun the chain of events that had brought everyone to this awful place?

"No, Mr. Kikowitz, I hope that won't be necessary. I'm glad Jason wasn't hurt. Where is he now?"

"He's at home of course—he's been suspended for the rest of the week, remember? Besides, why on earth would I let him back into school after a thing like this?"

"Believe it or not, I think school may be the best place for him right now. I might be able to arrange an in-school suspension given the circumstances. It would give me a chance to talk to him about all this."

Mr. Kikowitz snorted angrily. "I'm not about to send him."

"I understand. Please think it over and let me know if you change your mind." Some petty part of her wanted to remind Mr. Kikowitz that his son had been suspended for doing what had just been done to him—in all honesty, for doing even worse, since Jason had drawn blood.

It didn't have much effect. "I lay this at your doorstep, Ms. Browning. I expect some solution from you before the end of the day. That's the only consideration that will change my mind." His voice held no hint of cooperation or concern, just pure demand. She wondered if he barked orders like that to Jason every day. How fathers and sons could tangle each other into knots. Fathers and daughters, too.

The world was one giant ball of hurt and it wasn't

even 9:00 a.m. Heather picked up her keys and headed to the last place on earth she wanted to go: Max's cabin.

Chapter Eighteen

Max was just finishing his morning coffee when he heard a car pulling into the cabin parking lot. Seconds later his door banged open and JJ stalked into the kitchen.

"What is wrong with you? How could you possibly think that was a good idea?" Her eyes flashed in anger.

He didn't bother denying it. He hadn't even made any attempt to hide what they'd been doing last night, so he simply didn't say anything.

JJ sat down carefully, as if moving too fast would let her temper loose. "I've just come from a twenty-minute meeting—no, a twenty-minute department-wide *dressing down*—from Chief Bradens about a certain group of firefighters who roughed up Jason Kikowitz last night. Brian Williams came storming into the department this morning furious, and I don't blame him." She dropped her forehead into her hands.

"What are you doing? Reliving your glory days back in high school, shoving kids into lockers? This is beyond stupid, Max. *Irresponsible* doesn't even cover it. I'm—" she looked up at Max with sharp, angry eyes "—I'm ashamed to be your sister this morning."

He paused, making sure she was finished. "Not your brand of tactics—I get that." He didn't mind taking the heat for this. Not if it called dogs like Kikowitz off Simon. If having that kid's back knocked him off the "inspirational survivor" pedestal JJ and Alex kept shoving him on, then he'd gladly take the hit.

"What you don't get is how much damage you've done. To hear him talk, Simon Williams will be lucky Brian ever lets him out the door to pick up the mail now. Why didn't you just paint a bull's-eye on the back of his wheelchair, Max? Brian is convinced Simon is a walking target now, and I don't think he's wrong."

"Simon *isn't* walking. That's the whole point here."

She slammed her hands on the table. "Stop that!"

"Stop what?"

"Stop making everything about being in that chair. This has nothing to do with your injuries and everything to do with the kind of person I thought you were. *Were.* Because obviously I was wrong."

"You would have preferred I go over and have a deep, meaningful conversation with Jason Kikowitz?"

JJ stood up, bristling. "I would have preferred you act like an adult. I would have preferred you show Simon what it means to be a man instead of just another bully."

"Didn't the army teach you never to take a knife to a gunfight? The only way to deal with Kikowitz is to back him down, JJ. Simon couldn't do it, so I did it for him. Well, with a little help from some guys who were *all too happy* to give Kikowitz what he deserved. It's not like we beat the guy up or anything."

"Threats. You think threats were the way to go on this one?" She blinked at Max. "You think you stepped in on Simon's behalf. You don't even know how wrong you are on this, do you?"

Actually, he had known it on some level all along. It wasn't hard to go back to being the bad guy when he was so practiced at it. It took way too much energy to be a good guy with everyone staring at him. Luke Sullivan's "stop caring" attitude was gaining traction ever since he'd seen Mike Pembrose's post. The whole pipe dream of a future with Heather was a bubble that was bound to pop soon; he could see that now. Life only afforded guys like him certain benefits, and being upstanding didn't have to be one of them.

"Alex is on a plane right now or I'd tell him to come over here and fire you this minute. You're an idiot, Max, throwing away every good thing you've been given."

A sickening pity filled her eyes, and he hated that more than anything else she could say. "Oh, yeah, look at me, swimming in blessings."

He heard his front door open. "You *are,*" JJ said. "That's the worst part of it. If you'd only—"

She stopped talking as Heather walked silently into his kitchen.

"I think I'd better go now," JJ said quietly. "We're shorthanded at the station, since three guys just got suspended from duty for a week." She looked at Max. "Dishonorable conduct." She said the words as if pronouncing sentence on him.

Heather stood eerily still, her mouth drawn tight and her eyes cold. He wouldn't meet her glare, instead staring into his coffee and stirring it with a false indifference.

"Why?" It was more of a whisper, a moan, than a question.

"Because it had to be done."

"I can't think you believe that."

He leaned back in his chair. "Know me that well, do you?"

"I thought I did. Today, I'm not so sure."

Max didn't answer.

She took a step into the kitchen, and Max got a

whiff of whatever it was that made her hair smell so good. A tiny knife twisted in his gut. "Do you remember how I told Mrs. Williams I trusted you to do right by Simon?" She looked up and breathed in, doing that thing women did when they tried not to cry. The knife twisted harder. "I told her I believed in you. Do you know what it felt like to face her this morning? For me to agree with her that Simon should never spend time with you ever again?"

"Simon will be fine from here on in. Kikowitz will leave him alone. He doesn't need me."

"You think he'll be fine? You are so wrong. Simon's parents asked me about homeschooling him. They've decided the public school system can't meet his needs. That glass you think Simon is trapped under? It just came down hard and fast and airtight around him. I hope you're happy."

The anger—and yes, the regret—Max had been swallowing all morning roared up with a force too strong to stop.

He fought back with the only weapon he had. "As happy as you would have been with Mike Pembrose?"

Heather felt as if she'd been struck by lightning. Mike Pembrose? How had Mike been dragged into this? The shock of Max's question was instantly swallowed by a wave of regret. How could she think that what had happened with Mike would not follow her to Gordon Falls eventually? Wanting to put that sad chapter behind her was never the same thing as being able to escape it. She'd not made peace with that episode, and now she was paying the price.

"How do you know about Mike?" She hated how pain laced her words.

"I think the question is, why didn't you tell me about Mike?"

There wasn't a simple answer to that question. "He isn't part of my life anymore."

Max scrubbed a hand across his chin. "Yeah, you saw to that, didn't you?" He hadn't yet shaved, and the scruff gave him a regrettably rugged handsomeness she didn't want to notice. She'd come to Max's doorstep thinking life couldn't have tangled any further, and he'd proved her wrong.

She leaned against the counter, feeling slightly ill. A stronger woman would have been able to push back against this clear diversion, but this morning she wasn't that woman. "Tell me what you know."

Draining his coffee cup, Max gave her a hollow look. "Not much of a story. According to Mr. Pembrose, you found out he had diabetes and couldn't hack it. Did you give him the real reason you broke off the engagement? Or did you make up an excuse?"

It was so much more than that, but Heather wasn't

sure she was capable of explaining it to Max. Not in the middle of all this. The words wouldn't come.

"You can see how I might find this crucial information." Max's bitter tone sliced the air between them. "Since we're on the whole trust issue, as you say."

She shut her eyes. One black moment piling onto another—it seemed beyond unfair. "I can't discuss this now. Now has to be about Simon. Can you see that?"

"I'll talk to Simon. I'll explain why we did what we did, why Kikowitz will likely leave him alone now. His dad will come around."

"No." The one clear point in all this was that it had to stop. Here. Now. Before any more harm was done to anyone—including her. "You will not talk to Simon. Your relationship as his mentor is over. Your relationship—" she took a breath to steady her voice, feeling as if her throat were tying itself into knots "—with me is over. You are not to come to school." *To see me or Simon,* her broken heart added. "Simon's parents have forbidden you to contact him, so don't call or text him or go by the house."

"Well, I was getting too busy for all this anyhow." The worst thing of all was that Heather could see right through Max's act: he was applying that hard shell, pretending as if this were no big deal. His cavalier words couldn't mask the regret she saw pinching his features. The way his lips thinned and he swallowed harder. "I don't think he'll need my protection now anyways."

He needs your affection. She wanted to hate what Max had done. It was wrong in dozens of ways, and she had every right to be furious. But even all that couldn't wipe away the fact that Max had done it because he cared about Simon. It had come out in the worst possible way, but hadn't JJ said something about Max's spectacular gift for messing up? Hadn't she been warned?

"You won't lose your job or anything, right?" His voice pitched up just the slightest bit. "You had nothing to do with this."

"I don't know. I don't think so." She said the next words with more bitterness than she would have liked. "You're a grown man. No one expects me to control what you do on your own time off school property." After a second she felt compelled to add, "No, I think the big loser here will be Simon. You've managed to snatch back everything you gave him. I hope you can live with that."

Max pushed away from the table, spinning away from her under the pretense of putting the coffee creamer back in the refrigerator. He kept his hand on the handle for a long moment after he shut the door, knuckles whitening from how tightly he gripped.

Heather was nearly certain this would be the last time they spoke. She'd see him around town, of course, but there would be no more dances, no more dinners at The Black Swan or pie at Karl's. The knowledge gave her enough courage to speak her mind.

"Do you want to know why I broke it off with Mike?"

Max neither answered nor turned around, although he took his hand off the refrigerator handle and let it fall to his lap.

"Yes, I was scared when he shared his diabetes with me. I had spent so much time being the sick one that I was afraid I couldn't help anyone else through something so big for a whole life. So I admit that was part of it." Max's shoulders fell a bit, an "I knew it" gesture.

"But it wasn't all of it. Mike *became* his condition once he stopped hiding it from me. He let it rule him, let diabetes drive every aspect of his life for every minute. He complained constantly. He made me watch him take his insulin injections, moaned about what he couldn't eat, kept a list of side effects and complications in his wallet. There were conversations where he told people he was a diabetic before he introduced me as his fiancée. He lived in fear. He refused to have a family, afraid to pass along what he called 'the curse of his body' to our children. Mike chose to make himself a victim, and I knew I wasn't strong enough to marry a victim."

She almost didn't say it. But if this was going to

be her only chance, she didn't want to regret leaving it unsaid. "You are not a victim. That's what I'd hoped you would teach Simon. You were the strong one—you are determined to have all the life you can despite what's happened. I soaked that in, being close to you. I was starting to believe..." She let her voice trail off, and everything inside her wanted to crumple up into a ball of disappointment. Heather took a breath and made herself finish. "You're not a victim. Instead, you made Jason Kikowitz into a victim. And Simon. And me. So if you think that I'm walking away from you for the same reason I walked away from Mike, you couldn't be more wrong."

Chapter Nineteen

The door shut behind Heather, and Max's cabin felt bombed out, hollowed out, whatever was twelve times beyond empty. Times like these he most hated the limitations of his body. The urge to kick, to explode in a running, throwing rage couldn't be contained in arms and fists. He drew in angry, rumbling breaths, wanting to roar at something but having no target. This anger, this ticking time bomb of pent-up frustration was about to go off—had already gone off, if he really thought about it—and it needed speed and force to defuse. Speed and force—the very things he lacked.

He'd done the right thing. He alone knew Kikowitz needed a good scare, and he'd seen to it. That had to be true. The creeping doubt, the black regret that started in his stomach and seemed to feed on the looks in JJ's and Heather's eyes, that was sentimental nonsense. After all, no one was breaking down doors and shouting lectures at the other three from GFVFD.

Well, no one except Chief Bradens. Yeah, well, what did an upstanding do-gooder like Clark Bradens know about guys like Kikowitz? Thugs like he'd once been? People like Bradens, like Heather, they wouldn't last a day in his world. He was kidding himself if he thought he was anything but alone.

Alone. The word set fire to the exploding feeling again. Needing to smash something, Max took the empty coffee cup and hurled it to the floor. He wanted it to break into a thousand furious pieces, but the sturdy stoneware only bounced off the Formica, sending off one pathetic chip. He couldn't even reach down to pick it up and hurl it against something else.

It was good that Heather had ended it, no matter what she said. It hurt so much to watch her walk out that door now, it would have killed him if he'd gone ahead and fallen in love with her. He felt as if his heart was bound in barbed wire as it was. For the first time since the accident, Max wished he felt less instead of yearning to feel more.

There was one person who would understand what he was going through right now. Max scrolled though the contacts list on his cell until he found Luke Sullivan's number.

A woman's voice answered. "Hello?"

"Is Luke there?"

"Um...who is this please?" Whoever it was Luke had chosen as his companion for the night, she sounded decidedly unhappy.

"This is Max Jones. We're—" he groped for the right word "—business associates."

"Then you know Luke isn't in a position to talk right now." At Max's pause, she added, "I mean, you do know, right?"

"I'm not sure I follow you, Ms...."

"Sullivan. Terri Sullivan. I'm Luke's sister." He heard her let out a big breath. "Oh, man, you don't know, do you?"

"Know what?"

"Luke rolled his car Monday night. He was out drinking with some race buddies and he...well, he..." Her voice broke. "He's in a coma, okay? So it's not like he has time for business associates right now."

"I'm sorry." What else was there to say?

"Look, I gotta go. I... Well, I gotta go. I was supposed to be at the hospital ten minutes ago."

Max stared at the phone for a whole minute after the call ended. Sullivan's original injury had come from a drunk-driving accident. And now this. Some hero. Some champion. What a waste of a life.

Suddenly, the tiny cabin couldn't contain him. He needed space and speed, and there was only one place to really get it. In two minutes he'd grabbed a sweatshirt and was out the door, rolling down toward the docks and the *Sea Legs*. Who cared that it wasn't sailing weather? It was cold, but it was windy, and wind meant speed, wind meant power, and right now he needed as much of both as he could grab.

Max worked so fast to get himself into the boat, he nearly slipped twice in the process. Everything took so long in a chair! He slammed his seat into place with such force the whole boat shook; he yanked the dock lines fast enough to send them humming along the cleats, leaving friction burns on his palms. The pain felt good. Pain meant he was alive, meant that he was feeling something other than the anger.

The chilly late September wind sent the *Sea Legs* hurling through the river and whipped Max's hair hard against his face. Max pulled the sails in tighter, wrestling every bit of speed he could from the wind. The current put up a battle, but he welcomed it. He was itching for a fight. The craft sped across the water, up daringly on one keel, fast and feisty and satisfying.

His tension unraveled a notch with every mile, the speed and movement releasing the bristling ball of anger trapped in his chest. He took in a breath and yelled across the water, listening to the sound echo in the wide-open space. Gordon Falls and all its expectations faded behind him; the gray blustery sky ahead matched his thoughts. He bellowed again, just because it felt so good.

No matter how hard he tried, Max could not stop his thoughts from turning to Simon. Simon would never be allowed escapes like this. Stranded at home, surrounded by fear disguised as care, the kid would slowly and surely rot. He'd never know that life—even life in a chair—outlived high school, opening up beyond that tiny, petty world into a place where sports, camping, travel, jobs and all kinds of things awaited him. He'd probably never kiss a girl.

Kissing a girl was the most amazing thing. Kissing Heather had been like swallowing light, like drinking brilliance. Even now his neck remembered the feel of her hands. Even though relationships were off the table, Simon ought to know the exquisite sensation of a woman's hand slipping around his neck.

And you shoved her away.

The thought stabbed hard.

His retaliation to Kikowitz had nothing to do with Heather. He'd done it to protect Simon, not in some kind of psychobabble lash-out against intimacy. He hadn't sabotaged his relationship with Heather—it would have crashed on its own given time. Sure, this felt beyond lousy right now, but numbness was his gift in the world, wasn't it? What had Sullivan said? The first letdown feels like being dropped a mile?

A mile? Try ten miles. Try a thousand.

And now where was Sullivan? Lying in a hospital bed trying to stay alive. Again.

The boat shuddered and lurched, yanking Max from his thoughts to realize he'd come too close to shore and nearly beached the *Sea Legs* up on the muddy riverbank. He shook his head, pulled up the rudder a bit and luffed the sail enough to let the boat skid back into the deeper water. *Pay attention, Jones. Don't add stupid to stupid.*

You shoved her away. The convicting thought wouldn't go away. Max brought the boat about, returning it to its smooth speed through the river. He wanted to stop thinking, to outrun his thoughts and burn off his anger. Only he wasn't angry anymore. The wind and water had done their trick and tamped down the storm inside him. He just didn't like what was left.

You looked for reasons to leave her. You handed her a reason to leave you. Worse yet, you used Simon as your excuse to do it.

He could run this river all the way up to its source, and he wouldn't escape that conviction. On some level—maybe not then but certainly now—Max knew he'd helped orchestrate the revenge on Kikowitz because it would prove to Heather that he wasn't worth her affections. And that was so much easier that trying to live up to them, because that meant risking an eventual heartbreak.

The thought made him laugh. Max Jones, consummate risk taker, was running from risk. He pointed a finger at the blue heron standing gracefully in the shallows to his left. "That's right," he lectured the bird. "You know what those therapists say—pain is the mother of stupid. Fear is the father of stupid. And me, I've just been the prince of stupid, haven't I?" The bird only blinked and turned away as Max turned the boat back toward Gordon Falls.

He thought some sort of solution would come to him as he guided the boat back home. It didn't. He only knew he didn't want to be like Luke Sullivan, didn't want to keep everyone at a distance when that distance would eventually strangle him. Because while the world thought Luke had everything, it turned out Luke had nothing.

Now what? Max was pretty sure some whopping apologies were involved, only he didn't know quite how to make that happen. Truth was, he still wasn't sorry for getting to Kikowitz, just sorry for the fallout. And he was still terrified of getting in too deep with Heather only to learn she couldn't handle life with a paraplegic. Only he was also just as terrified of losing her, which he was pretty sure he'd just done.

How fair was it that Alex, the master problem solver and the guy who said he was on Max's side, was in San Francisco for the week? This was not the kind of thing to handle in text messages and continually dropped cell-phone calls. *Great*. He scowled to himself. *Now where do I go?*

Max nearly groaned aloud when he turned the boat about to see the gleaming white steeple of Gordon Falls Community Church poking above the fall foliage like some kind of sign someone had put there. "Aw, come on, really? That's a bit Hollywood, isn't it?" Max asked the sky.

He knew what JJ would say. He knew what Alex would say. For that matter, he was pretty sure what Heather would say.

The words of one of his therapists rang in his head. *If you think you're going to fall, grab on to the nearest sturdy thing.*

Well, okay, Lord, Max tentatively informed God as he tied the boat up. *This is me grabbing.*

Thursday morning, Heather stared at the vicious orange letters spray painted onto the sidewalk in front of Simon Williams's house. Graffiti of any kind—much less the hateful outburst this displayed—seemed so out of place in quaint Gordon Falls. It shouted at her from the sidewalk. It poked at her from the fingers of the neighbors who pointed and stared. It pummeled her from the wounded look in Simon's mother's eyes as she peered out their living room window.

Someone—and it didn't take a genius to figure out who—had painted *gimp* on the sidewalk. She wondered if Jason Kikowitz had known the slur was viewed among the worst in the disability community—something so cruel it could barely be said by one person with a disability to another and could never be used by an able-bodied person. Had he known and wielded that? Or had it been a terrible happenstance?

Oh, Lord, how could You allow this to go so far? Her mother often employed the term *heartsick*. She told Heather she was "heartsick" over how things had deteriorated after the driver of her accident seemed to go unpunished. She'd been "heartsick" at how Dad let the injustice of it consume him. Heather was heartsick now. Unbearably heartsick at how a situation that had once been so filled with promise now compounded sorrow upon regret upon destruction. *It's all gone so horribly wrong, Lord. You're going to have to show me what to do because I truly don't know.*

The fire chief's red truck pulled up the street, and Chief Bradens's eyes looked as bad as she felt. Three other men got out of the truck and began pulling equipment out of the back. "The boys are here to power-wash that off the sidewalk. I've already talked to the police because I think these three ought to be the ones to scrub it off."

Heather thought she knew why, but she asked anyway. "Those three?"

"I'm sorry to say those three louts were the ones

to rattle Jason Kikowitz's cage the other night. Well, them and someone JJ is probably yelling at again right about now. If you'll excuse me."

Chief Bradens walked his men up to the front door. She saw Brian wave his arms angrily, pointing at the three young men who had the good sense to look ashamed of themselves. The door slammed shut. Chief Bradens shook his head with the same disappointed frustration she'd been feeling and ordered the crew to get to work.

She looked up to offer Simon a friendly wave— just the smallest show of support—but the shades had been drawn. Sighing, Heather walked up to the door and rang the bell. It might do more harm than good, but she couldn't just stand there and not at least try to reach out to Simon.

Mrs. Williams was slow to come to the door, opening it only far enough to show her face. "Morning."

"I was wondering if maybe Simon would like to talk."

She didn't look too keen on the idea.

"Or," Heather tried, "at least I'd like the opportunity to tell him how sorry I am about all that's happened. Please."

"Let her in, Mom," Simon called from somewhere behind the door.

Mrs. Williams reluctantly opened the door wider and gestured Heather inside. Simon was in the living room of the tidy home, slumped on a recliner while his chair stood empty in a corner of the room. He looked like every other fifteen-year-old boy in the world sprawled on the chair like that, boasting a T-shirt and jeans and playing with some electronic device he had on his lap.

Heather sat down in the chair nearest him. Mrs. Williams stood in the archway to the room, arms crossed, watching.

"Mom…" Simon whined, glaring at his mom. "You mind?"

To Heather's surprise, Mrs. Williams unfolded her hands. "I'll be in the kitchen getting lunch started if you need me." She gave Heather an "I'm watching you" glare before she left the room.

Simon switched off the game and tossed it on the coffee table. "They're beyond mad, you know. I've never seen Dad so worked up."

Heather couldn't believe Simon's tone of voice. "They have every right to be. What happened was horrible. I'm really, really sorry."

"Yeah, well, that's high school. One rotten day after another. Mom grounded me for getting detentions, which is pretty funny, since she never lets me go anywhere anyway. Kinda dumb."

"I wish you were coming back." It was true. Even though she could understand the Williamses' decision, she felt as if high school had so much to offer

Simon. She believed things could get better, even though she had no idea how.

Simon shot a look toward the kitchen. "You and me both. Homeschool? Puh-lease."

Heather didn't know what to say. She'd expected Simon to want to stay home, not return to the scene of his torment. "You want to come back?"

Simon waved his hands around the room. "Would you want to spend all day in here? With them?"

The home was lovely, and his parents spared no effort on his behalf. How very like a teenager to find such an environment intolerable. "What about Kikowitz?"

"He's a jerk. I hate him." Evidently Simon didn't see what that had to do with it. He held up his phone. "I got a text from Candace. She told me she felt bad about letting it slip to Jason, that he'd sort of pulled it out of her when she hadn't meant to say anything. She said she'd understand if I didn't want to help her with her algebra anymore, but that she'd be really glad if I still could." He shot Heather a knowing glance. "She got another D. Really, it's not that hard—the girls in my class seem to get it okay."

"Simon." Heather tried to hide her astonishment. "Aren't you upset by what's happened?"

"Sure I am. It rots. Kikowitz is a jerk." He leaned in. "And I gotta say, Max is kind of a jerk, too. I mean, it's nice that the guys tried to help me out and all, but even I could have told him something like this was gonna happen. Aren't adults supposed to know better? My parents will never let me play hockey now."

"Yes." Heather could not help but laugh. "Adults are supposed to know better." In many ways Simon was already so much wiser than his years. "I'm glad to know you see Max's response wasn't the right one."

"It was kinda cool but sorta stupid. How many other freshmen have henchmen?"

Maybe Simon wasn't as wise as she thought. "Henchmen?"

"That's what Dad called them. Well—" the boy smirked "—Dad called them lots of things, but he said they were no better than some villain's henchmen, getting revenge on the bad guy by being bad themselves."

"Your father is right, but I think *henchmen* is going a bit far." *That's Max Jones,* she thought. *Always going a bit too far and luring others to do the same.*

"I see it like this. When a mean kid trips and falls in the lunchroom, you know you shouldn't enjoy it, but you do. You know what I mean?"

"Simon, revenge is a really slippery business." She thought of her father and how the pursuit of justice had slid so easily into the craving for revenge. She'd found and read some of Max's earliest press statements from his accident, and she'd seen the same dangerous hunger in his words. She thought Max had grown beyond it; she knew her father had buried himself in it and now she wondered if her role here was to ensure Simon never went there at all. She scooted her chair closer. "I know you go to church, so I know you understand that God needs to play a part in how you handle all this. Your response to all this has to come from who you are, not who Jason is. Or who Max is. Or even who your parents are."

Simon shrugged his shoulders. "Pastor Allen was here this morning—Mom and Dad called him right after they called the police and school. He said pretty much the same thing. About me, that is—he left out the part about Mom, Dad and Max."

"Well, Simon, what do you want to do about all this?"

Simon slumped back against the chair cushions. "I want it all to go away. I just want to go to chemistry and Ping-Pong Club and have it all go away."

Heather slumped back against her own chair. "I hear you on that one."

Simon raised an eyebrow at her. "You're really ticked at him, aren't you?"

"Who? Jason? You bet I am."

"No, Max. I heard my mom telling my dad how you told her she could trust Max to be a good influence and all. Sorta botched that one, didn't he?"

Heather remembered thinking once that Simon

might have a good deal to teach Max. "Yes, he missed it by a mile."

"He's still figuring it out, I guess. He's been in his chair, what, a year? I've been in mine my whole life. We've gotta give him time."

Heather smiled. "How old are you again, Simon?"

He grinned. "Sixteen in December."

She gave his hand a squeeze, and he groaned and flinched like every other teenage boy she'd ever known. "No, you're not. You're much, much older than that." She stood up, a silent prayer of thanks that God had made her path clear. "Do you really want to come back to school?"

"Better than being cooped up at home, even with Kikowitz."

"Okay, then. I'll see what I can do."

Chapter Twenty

"Mom?" Heather gripped the phone tightly.

"Heather? It's Thursday. Aren't you in school?"

She sank into the couch. "I'm not going in today."

"Honey? Are you all right?"

"No." What was the point of hiding it? "I mean I'm fine—physically—but I need some advice."

Heather could hear her mother settle into her chair. "All right, then, what about?"

"Did you ever get to the point where you could forgive Dad for the way he behaved after I got hurt? I mean, did it ever get better with him, or between you?"

She heard Mom suck in a breath. "That's a big question. Maybe it would help if you tell me why you're asking."

Heather spilled out the whole story. In between fits of crying and anger, she chronicled the stormy progression from choosing Max as Simon's mentor to the horrors of what had been scrubbed from Simon's sidewalk. "I'm hurt. Simon's hurt. The fire department is hurt. I think even Jason Kikowitz is hurt. Mom, this went from bad to amazing to worse so fast I can't figure out what to do."

"Oh, honey, I'm so sorry you've been tangled up in such a mess. It hardly seems fair. You've had more than your share of this kind of thing already between Mike and your dad. I had no idea things had gotten so…personal…between you and this Max fellow."

Heather sank farther into the couch cushions, suddenly exhausted. "It sort of crept up on me. How can someone be so wonderful and then so horrible?"

Her mother's sigh held so much regret. "I asked that about your father so many times. He loved you so much. He would do anything for you. But your accident seemed to bring out something…I don't know…raw and angry inside him. Something that became bigger than him, something that swallowed up all the love inside him even though I think it was born out of his love for you." She paused before adding, "Yes, I forgave him, but it was a long time before I could."

Heather was hoping for something that would feel more like a solution. Instead, her mother's words made her feel as though she were living in a continual cycle of the same problem. As if injury, disease and their aftermath would haunt her the rest of her life.

"Why do you think Max did what he did? Did he tell you?"

"He thought he was standing up for Simon. Letting the bully kid know that there were bigger, stronger bullies who would defend Simon. He said he thought it had to be done, and he'd take the heat for it so that Simon wouldn't be a target again. Only he's just made Simon a bigger target—and let all of us down in the bargain. How can he claim to care about me and do something like this when he knew I was trusting him with Simon?" She grabbed a tissue off the coffee table as the tears started up again. "How, Mom?"

"He went about it all wrong, absolutely. But even I know that people lash out when something precious to them is threatened. I'm not making excuses, but it may be that Max wasn't quite ready for how much he'd come to care about you and Simon."

"He picked the worst way to show it."

"Oh, I agree. But even your father's vengeance began with his deep love for you. Your father just kept on going down the sinkhole, getting darker and darker. Seems to me Max will either wake up to what he's done and try to set it right, or he'll head down a sinkhole of his own."

"What do I do?" Her words sounded like a little girl's whine.

"I don't know that there's much you *can* do right now. Try to be there for Simon—do what's best for him. Pray. If Max is the man you think he might be, he'll own up to how he's hurt you. Your heart will tell you what to do then."

"What if it tells me to walk away? Like I did to Mike?"

"You know why you left Mike. Don't start doubting that decision just because it's come on you again. You are a survivor, Heather. You've healed from more than most people your age. God would not want you with someone who will hurt you. I'm certain what Max does next will tell you what you need to know. But I'll still pray." Her mom's voice took on the edge of tears now, too. "I've never stopped praying. I'm so proud of you. You know that?"

"I do, Mom. Thanks."

Heather set down the phone and echoed her Mom's advice. "Okay, Max Jones. The ball's in your court." She remembered the way Max had flung himself out of his chair to make Simon feel better that afternoon they had played Ping-Pong, and her heart twisted. *Get through to him, Lord. He could be so wonderful.*

"Will you tell him to give me a call or stop by the cabins?" Max handed the church secretary a card, feeling naive for expecting Pastor Allen to be free and available whenever a sorry soul came waltzing into church in need. God probably only worked like that in the movies. Then again, when that steeple had appeared in his sights, all lit in sunshine like a neon arrow pointing "Go here"…

A thought struck him. "Hey, what's the name of that older lady from the knitting group, the short one, kinda feisty? Her name starts with a *V,* I think…"

"Violet Sharpton?"

"Yes, her. Are you allowed to give me her phone number?"

"I won't need to. She's just down the hall in the church library. You can go talk to her yourself."

Max found himself not entirely ready to put this particular plan into action. Still, he'd heard the knitting ladies talk about how shawls were best for times when words wouldn't do, and he knew he didn't have the words to apologize to Heather. He'd hoped that talking with the pastor would help him find the words…but maybe he could show his remorse in another way. Max wheeled himself out of the office in the direction the secretary had pointed, trying not to think that maybe Pastor Allen wasn't available just so Violet Sharpton could hear his outrageous request. *I'm not ready to be one of JJ's "God appointments."*

When he turned into the library, Mrs. Sharpton was standing at a table stacked high with children's books.

"Hot Wheels! You're the last person I expected to see today. How are you, Max?"

How to answer that? "I'm in a bit of hot water, Mrs. Sharpton, and I think I might need your help."

She whipped off her glasses and came around to his side of the table. "Well, now, that's a mighty intriguing answer. Let me sit down and you can tell me what's up."

At first he yearned to spill out the whole story, but he decided some of the details weren't quite public and perhaps it was time to show a little discretion for a change. "I've done something that's hurt Heather Browning, and I'd like to ask you to make a special prayer shawl as my way of apologizing."

The older woman folded her hands. "Oh, my. That sounds serious."

"I suppose it is." Max cast his eyes around the room, suddenly self-conscious. This was a silly, mushy idea and he shouldn't be here. And yet it also seemed like the perfect gesture. "It's…it's not something I can easily fix. As a matter of fact, it might not be something I can fix at all, which is why I think the shawl might be a good idea."

"Means that much to you, does she?"

The older woman was making grand assumptions, but her eyes were so amused he found he couldn't get angry. "Well, I don't really know yet, Mrs. Sharpton."

She waved his denial away with a *tsk*. "Call me

Vi. And of course you know. You wouldn't be here with your face so red if you didn't." She gave him a "fess up" look that would have had him sinking guiltily into a chair if he wasn't already in one. "What did you do, son?"

He really didn't want to go into it. Then again, if Gordon Falls worked the way everyone said it did, everyone would know before the end of the day anyhow. He told her the shortest version of recent events he could manage.

"Well, now, I don't know what to say." She planted her thin little hands on her hips. "Half of me wants to clap you on the back for giving that hooligan a what for, and the other half wants to knock you upside the head for showing such a poor example. What ever made you think that was a smart idea?"

Before he realized it, Max had spilled the whole business about Mike Pembrose and the speech Luke Sullivan had given him. He hadn't even told most of that to JJ, so he had no idea why it all came out to this little gray-haired spitfire of a woman who somehow seemed kind and chastising at the same time. "I think we're pretty much a lost cause, Heather and I, and that's for the best. Still, I feel like I have to do something and not leave it like this."

Vi sat back in her chair, folding her arms across her chest. "So, you've decided it's a lost cause, have you? Better to not give Heather a chance to let you down than to risk taking it any further. That Luke Sullivan was right all along, you think."

Well, when you put it that way... Max shrugged, at a loss for an answer.

Violet Sharpton reached out and whacked him on the head. "Luke Sullivan is dead wrong, young man! And where he is right now ought to prove it to you!"

"Ouch!" Max couldn't quite believe the woman had such a left hook.

"I'm glad that hurt. You need to wake up. You're not afraid she'll leave you—you're afraid she *won't!*" She addressed the ceiling—or God, Max wasn't quite sure which. "What's the matter with young people today, wanting life all tied up in pretty bows with all the problems solved?"

"I hardly think my life is all tied up in—"

"Don't interrupt me, Hot Wheels. I'm just getting started. You got hurt bad—I get that. Lots of men I know wouldn't be able to pull themselves out of a hole like that, much less with your admirable sense of panache. You've got a right to be angry—but only for a while and not at the whole world. Heather Browning could be the best thing that's ever happened to you. Only I think you already know that. So step up to the plate, son—or wheel up to it, in your case—and grab at a chance with her. You will not regret it even if she does break your heart in the end because *you will have given it a shot.*"

She grabbed his hand, shaking it with each word. "And that's what matters." Her eyes teared up a bit, making Max wonder what in life had given her all that fire.

"I'll bet Mr. Sharpton is an awesome guy."

Her expression gave Max the answer. "He was, honey. He truly was."

Had his parents ever loved each other like that? Fierce and full of life? He'd never heard Mom talk about Dad that way. Alex and JJ had that maybe, but it was still so new for them. At the end of it all, he wanted what Vi had had. Anything else wouldn't feel like enough. "I'm sorry for your loss."

She sniffed. "Don't be sorry. Be telling me what color yarn to buy."

"Do you think you could pull off pink with flamingos?"

Her smile sparkled, even with the tears still brimming in her eyes. "After your flamethrower, I can do *anything*."

Max rolled past the church office ten minutes later. "You can tell Pastor Allen he doesn't need to call me back."

The secretary looked up, baffled. "Are you sure?"

"Yep. Violet Sharpton just took me to church."

Chapter Twenty-One

Margot stood in Heather's office doorway Friday morning. "Mrs. Williams just sent me an email formally requesting Simon's withdrawal from school." Margot never sugarcoated bad news. While Heather knew that—and often liked that about her—she wished for a softer blow this morning.

"After all that conversation yesterday? All Simon's pleading?" She'd spent several hours after school yesterday helping Simon tell his parents he didn't want to stay home. She felt the failure settle around her like a lead wrapping. Margot was right—this had become a deeply personal battle for her.

"They are his parents. It's their decision."

Heather pushed away her keyboard and sunk her chin into her hands. "What do you think?"

Margot leaned against the doorway and sighed. "I think Simon is becoming his own person, and that's good. But that person is still only fifteen and may not know what's best right now. There's always next year. Or even next semester."

"That doesn't help. I hate it that Kikowitz wins. Why does he get to come back to school and rule the lunchroom while Simon sits at home?"

"Coach Mullen suspended him from the play-offs, if that makes you feel any better."

Heather raised a doubtful eyebrow. "It should, but it doesn't."

Margot folded her hands in front of her in an "it is what it is" gesture. "Well, we've still got curriculum night to get through and I—" She caught sight of something in the hallway that stopped her mid-sentence. "I'm going to leave you to your visitor."

"My visitor?"

Max wheeled into the administrative offices, a serious look seeming foreign on his usually cavalier features.

Margot caught Heather's eye. "Unless you need me to stay?"

"No," Heather said quietly. Even after everything that had happened, how could she still be so drawn in by Max's presence? "I'm okay."

"You're sure?"

She nodded. Max, who still had not said a word, wheeled silently into her office. She let him nudge the guest chair aside, needing to keep her desk between them. "I asked you not to come to school."

"I know you did. But I can't get up the stairs to your apartment and I wasn't sure you'd come down to meet me if I called."

He was right; she probably wouldn't have. He still tugged at her heart in ways she wasn't strong enough to resist. How fair was it that he seemed twice as compelling now as he had when he was all boastful and defiant?

"This is for you." He placed a small package on her desk rather than handing it directly to her. She was glad of that—she didn't want to risk any touch from him right now. "Well, sort of. It's not really a gift, more of an...offering."

Intrigued, she picked up the package and pulled open the brown paper wrapping. Inside was the Never Apologize shirt she'd seen him wear multiple times. *Really?* That was his idea of an offering? As far as she was concerned, Max owed her a handful of apologies.

"I can't wear it anymore. Mostly because you're about to become the first person I've apologized to in years. I hurt you. I betrayed your trust in me, and I hurt Simon." He waited until she looked up at him before adding, "I'm sorry. I know it probably doesn't change anything, but I am sorry."

He was right; it didn't change anything. Part of her was glad he didn't go so far as to ask for her forgiveness, because she wasn't ready to give it. "Simon wants to come back to school but his parents just requested he be withdrawn for homeschooling. I tried to change their minds, but I failed."

"He wants to come back, after all that, but they won't let him?" The old defiant Max appeared in the narrowing of his eyes.

She parroted Margot's words. "It's their decision. He's their son." After a moment, she added, "And we haven't given them a lot of reasons to place their confidence in us to keep him safe." Some wounded part of her wanted to snap, *Thanks to you,* but she didn't. Max was the catalyst, surely, but he wasn't the whole problem. "Even if Kikowitz is expelled, I couldn't hope to assure them some other bully wouldn't pick up where he left off."

"That's not a reason. Life is full of Kikowitzes."

"Maybe it *is* best. Simon is so bright—he'll probably be ready for college courses by his sophomore year if he homeschools. The state college would be so much more welcoming to him than we could ever be."

He frowned at her. "You don't believe that."

She was trying to, if only to soften the sting of failing Simon. "It's not my choice."

Max ran his hands down his face. "So now what?"

"There isn't anything to do, Max." All that was left now was to slosh her way through the aftermath and pray that some good came out of the month Simon had been at school. She couldn't bear the thought that all this had come to nothing at all.

"*I* don't believe *that*."

She held up the shirt. "Then, if you want something to do, I think you should go apologize to Simon and his parents. If there's one thing you can still teach Simon, it's how a man behaves when he's wrong." She stunned herself with the force of her words.

"I doubt they'll let me."

She stood up. "Then simply let Simon see you try."

She expected Max to huff *Fine!* and wheel from the room. Instead he looked up at her with something she'd never seen in his eyes before and asked, "Will you come with me?"

It was a long, unsteady moment before she replied. "Yes."

Max had flung himself off a cliff at night in the rain and not been as anxious as he was now. Of course, he had been a different man before that night, caring about different things and not caring about a lot of things. Somehow—and Max still wasn't quite sure how—this whole business with Simon and Heather had become a tipping point. As he wheeled past the faint orange lettering still visible on the sidewalk in front of the Williamses' house, Max knew big things were riding on the outcome of today.

"Hello." Brian Williams's eyes were as icy as his

tone when he pulled open the front door. While the ramp built for Simon made it logistically easy to go inside, the invisible obstacles felt like Mount Everest. Max couldn't be certain if he'd be allowed to stay ten seconds after offering his apology, but he was going to try.

"Good afternoon, Mr. Williams." Max held out a hand, but Mr. Williams declined to shake it. It was a painful reminder of the time just after his accident when Alex Cushman had extended a hand to him, and he'd been the one to refuse the courtesy. That vengeful first meeting with Alex had eventually led to a business partnership—and a family connection now that Alex was JJ's husband. Max let that truth carry him past Brian's cold greeting and keep his optimism. *Time,* as Alex was fond of saying, *for God to show how big He is.*

"Hi, Simon. Hello, Mr. and Mrs. Williams." Heather managed to keep her tone light and cheerful even though Max knew she'd caught the father's gesture.

Max moved his attention to Simon's mother, who perched nervously on the living room couch. "I want to thank you for letting me come, Mrs. Williams. I know this wasn't easy."

She simply nodded, worrying the end of her sweater between her fingers.

"Hey, kid." Max bumped his fist against Simon's. The gesture lacked Simon's usual enthusiasm, but

Simon also didn't share his parents' frowns, so that was something. "I hope it's okay that I brought you a present." The gift had been Alex's idea, and since his boss was an acknowledged master of communication, Max had taken the advice.

The package produced a small smile from Simon. "Whoa! These are sick." He extracted a set of fingerless leather gloves—the kind preferred by wheelchair athletes. The flame motif was just an added bonus.

Heather leaned toward Mrs. Williams. "'Sick' is good, just in case you were wondering." Max was sure that would get a laugh, but it didn't.

"Try them on. I think I got the size right." He wheeled closer to Simon and helped the boy wiggle his hands into the fierce-looking gloves. "The grip is outstanding. I got these from a wheelchair rugby team, and those guys are very picky about their gloves. They should let you crush your opponents at the Ping-Pong table." He regretted that last remark. Simon wasn't likely to play Ping-Pong if he didn't go back to school. Maybe he'd ask Alex to help him find a way to get a table donated to the church youth group.

"Thanks." Simon flexed his fingers and then wobbled in his usual slow, precarious gait over to the chair in the corner of the room. The fact he could walk even short distances was going to make life so much easier for Simon. So many more things were possible for him—it doubled Max's conviction to keep him out in the world. When Simon slipped into the chair and popped enough of a wheelie to make his mother groan, Max could only smile.

Heather caught Max's eye, nodding. It was time to do what he came to do.

"Mr. and Mrs. Williams, I'd like to offer you an apology for my role in what happened. I had the chance to stop the business with Jason Kikowitz, and instead I let how much I like Simon cloud my better judgment." He directed his next words to Simon. "I wanted to protect you, and I went about it in exactly the wrong way. And you paid for it." He looked back at Simon's parents. "You all paid for it. I was supposed to be showing Simon the right way to act, and I did the furthest thing from it." The next part was hardest of all. "I'm sorry—really sorry— and I hope you'll find your way to forgiving me someday." Apologizing went against Max's nature, but asking for forgiveness felt like ripping his skin off and sitting there like an open wound. The resulting silence in the room made Max want to squirm.

"You were hugely stupid to do that."

"Simon!" Mrs. Williams chided her son's pronouncement.

"No, he's right." Max looked at Simon, newly amazed by this kid. "It *was* a supremely stupid thing to do, and I'm glad you see it that way. I wanted Kikowitz to know the guys and I had your back and that he couldn't rough you up without consequences. Only 'thugging' him wasn't the right way to do it. I let you down, I behaved like a two-year-old, and I'm sorry. But we do have your back, Simon. Know that."

"Thank goodness you don't have to go back there." Mr. Williams spoke for the first time. Simon's whole body reacted to the statement. It didn't take a counseling degree to read the body language in the room: Mr. Williams was set on Simon's withdrawal, Simon was against it and Mrs. Williams was caught somewhere in the middle.

"I want to go back there, Dad." Simon popped another small wheelie with a little rock back and forth at the top. Max was proud Simon had mastered the trick, but found this a counterproductive moment for hotdogging.

"How on earth can you want to go back there?" Mrs. Williams's tone was filled with a mother's worry.

"It's high school. Okay, it's not perfect, but there's lots of stuff I like. Things I can do. Friends I can spend time with."

Girls, Max added silently.

"You have friends at youth group. And no one's going to start fights with you there."

"I was hoping," Heather offered in a careful tone, "that we might find some sort of compromise."

"With all due respect, Ms. Browning, we've already seen how little you can do to protect my son. I think it's best we call this experiment to an end and count our blessings there was no real harm done."

"The real harm is that I get stuck at home when I could be at school." Simon sounded as put out as any teen Max had ever heard. With an insolent glare straight at his dad, he added, "Like *normal* kids."

"Simon, I'm thirsty." Heather stood up. "Can you show me where to get a glass of water in your kitchen?" Max guessed she was trying to salvage the conversation before Simon goaded his parents into an all-out battle. Max saw more of his own personality in Simon than he'd ever expected that first day the boy had wheeled meekly into the gym.

The air grew thick as Heather and Simon left the room. This kind of diplomacy was so far out of Max's skill set that he found himself throwing up a panicked *Help!* to heaven. He tried to meet Mrs. Williams's eyes, but she looked down at her hands.

Mr. Williams simply glared at him. "Simon has changed." It was crystal clear where he placed that blame.

"Simon is growing up. He's trying to figure out who he is, and that means who he is apart from you. I was the same—actually, I was ten times worse—in high school." When that met with no reception, Max plowed on. "I think the world of your son. He's smart and so much tougher than he looks. There are so many things he could do, so much stuff out there for him to try and explore."

"It's our job to protect Simon. Surely you can see that." Mrs. Williams folded her hands in her lap.

"I get that. I know I'm not a parent, and I'm not even two years out from my injury, but I do understand." Max ran his hands down his face, straining for the right words. "But what I hope you understand is that life is filled with Kikowitzes. Guys who will single Simon—or even me—out as the weak target and pounce. Don't you want Simon to know how to handle it? Don't you want him to be able to go out into the world, go to college, have a job, travel, all that stuff?"

"Of course we want Simon to have a rich and full life."

"Then maybe the best time and place for him to learn how to handle guys like Kikowitz is now, in school, where he's got loads of support and guidance." Max leaned in, determined to put every ounce of persuasion he had into the moment. "He's so, so smart. He'll get knocked down—I know that—but Simon will get back up. Come on—he already has. He told you he wants to go back. You've gotta let him."

"You have a lot of nerve telling us what we have to do after the way you've acted." Mr. Williams crossed his arms over his chest.

The old Max would have pounced on that. Today,

Max knew Brian Williams was absolutely correct. "You're right. I've got no say in this. Except that the last months I've spent out in the real world, away from the nice supportive cocoon of rehab, have taught me how tough it is to get by. It's hard. Some days it's really hard." Max shifted his gaze to Mrs. Williams, hoping the soft spot he had for Simon would come through in his words. "But I look at Simon and I see a kid who has what it's going to take. He's got so much more confidence than he did even a month ago. He's got parents who would do anything for him. He's got enough wit to defuse a situation when someone is a jerk, and soon enough he'll have the experience to know how and when to use that wit instead of a right hook or a well-rammed footrest. Please don't let my lack of good sense keep Simon from staying out there in the world."

"Your son stood up to a bully." Heather's voice came from the entryway. "That takes strength. I know he didn't do it the way we all would have liked—"

"You've all made *that* clear!" Simon shouted from the kitchen, proving the walls had ears.

"But he stood up for himself nonetheless. He's also bearing the consequences with a fair amount of maturity—"

"I'm grounded for life—did you know that?" Simon's dramatic declaration bellowed from the kitchen. Max tried not to grin. He'd been grounded any number of lifetimes.

"With as much maturity as you can expect at fifteen." Heather finally finished her thought. "I can't say that about too many students these days."

"We'll think about what you've said," Mrs. Williams offered.

"I think we're finished here." Mr. Williams declared the visit over.

Max headed toward the door, shooting Simon a wave as he went by the kitchen. "See you around?"

Simon shrugged. "Um, 'grounded for life,' remember?"

Max mimed texting on a cell phone, raising one eyebrow. "They take away your phone?"

Simon shook his head. "Nobody's that cruel."

Max gave Simon a thumbs-up and rolled out the door, hoping that wasn't the last time he'd see Simon Williams.

Chapter Twenty-Two

Max sat at his desk Monday, completely unable to work, willing his cell phone to ring. It had been two whole days since he'd laid his conscience bare in front of the Williams family, and the lack of response was eating him alive. Simon's future had become deeply, personally important to him, and his passion for the boy's opportunities lay foreign and unsettling in his stomach.

"I'd always expected I'd catch your passion for the whole world—the 'getting guys with disabilities out into experiences' thing—but not in terms of one scrawny, brilliant kid." Max was glad Alex was in the office today, because he needed to talk this out with someone or he'd explode. "The need to make this right is driving me nuts."

As soon as the words left his mouth, Max realized how close to home that urge must feel to Alex. His boss and brother-in-law had talked many times about his old company's role in making the climbing line Max had been using when he fell. Max was here and had the amazing job he did because of Alex's persistent need to "put things right." Okay, falling for JJ may have amplified that a bit, but Max's tumult was tangled up with Heather, too.

"Who'd have guessed we'd end up with so much in common?" Alex said with a quiet smile, then pointed up and added, "Well, except for you know who." He walked over and perched on the corner of Max's desk, picking up the drawings of new "Maxed Out" lightning-bolt wheel panels that would be in the company's next catalog. "I boast I know how to think outside the box, but the Good Lord blew me out of the water on this one."

"Yeah."

Alex raised an eyebrow. "Yeah?"

Usually Max dismissed any of Alex's continual comments about how God had paved the way for this whole venture, but he knew too much now to ignore how God had intervened in his life. If anyone understood what he was going through, it was Alex. Alex, who at one point was his enemy, the man he'd set out to crush. If that wasn't evidence of God and grace in his life, what was?

"Heather said something to me one night. It's stuck with me, working on me until I could actually, well, believe it." He ran his hands through his hair, trying to put that moment into words.

Alex set the drawings down. "What?"

"The night that whole thing blew up with Simon and his parents—the first time, I mean—I got frustrated enough to spit out to Heather that I was furious at God for letting me fall." These words were hard to say to Alex, but they'd long had to learn to be honest with each other. "For dropping me."

He could see the impact of the words in Alex's eyes. There were people who insisted it was Alex's company's climbing line that had failed Max. Max no longer felt that to be true. Lots of things were to blame for what had happened that night, but none more than Max's own arrogance. Alex's silence spoke of the whole hard journey the past year and a half had been for everyone.

"Heather said the most amazing thing when I blurted that out." Max made a point to look straight at Alex, wanting him to see that it had gone beyond hurt and blame, wanting him to believe the healing Max knew was taking place. "She said…" Max remembered the unbelievable tenderness in Heather's tone and the words suddenly caught in his throat. "She said she believed God caught me just in time."

Alex's eyes closed for a moment, and Max knew the words were just as powerful for him. "You hang on to that woman, Max Jones. She's a keeper."

Max was planning to tell Heather just what she'd done that night when he got the chance to give her the prayer shawl Violet Sharpton had made. "I'm trying, Alex. There's a mile of hurt between us right now—and I put most of it there—but I'm fighting it with everything I've got. She came with me to talk to Simon and his parents, so that's something." He sunk his head onto his hands. "This is so hard."

Alex rested a hand on his shoulder. "You've done a million near-impossible things since I've met you, Max. I'm pretty sure you can pull this off." He spun his wedding ring with his thumb. "Some things are worth fighting for with all you've got. I'm pretty sure Heather's one of them." He gave Max's shoulder a squeeze before letting go. "Although I wouldn't mind if you at least *tried* to do battle with next year's sponsorship schedule."

Max despised paperwork. Alex could whip up plans and spreadsheets and timetables with his eyes closed, but that kind of forethought was like a foreign language to Max. "It's late—I know." He groaned. "If just one of them—Simon or Heather or even Brian Williams—would call me I'd be able to think straight, you know?"

"Yeah," Alex commiserated. "I do know. But try anyway."

Max wrestled with the spreadsheet for over an hour, and even the addition of an extra-strong coffee from down the street hadn't bolstered his success. He was just about to slam something hard into his computer monitor when his cell phone rang. With a wide smile he saw Heather's name on the screen.

"Are you sitting down?"

Some part of him was overjoyed that she could make such a joke. The caution and careful nature of their conversations lately jangled his nerves. "As a matter of fact, I am. Good guess."

"I had two visitors this morning."

Please, Lord, let one of them be Simon. Please. The prayer slipped out of Max with unexpected ease. "You did?"

"Linda Williams came in this morning. She wanted to know if we could hold a place for Simon for the second semester."

Max felt the illogical sensation of his heart both leaping and falling at the same time. "You mean in January? Not now?" It didn't feel like enough of a victory.

His words must have echoed his frustration. "I think it's a good compromise, Max. It gives everyone a chance to catch their breath and keeps the door open for Simon to come back. And it wouldn't be happening at all if it weren't for you." The tone of her voice changed completely, now soft and low. "Thank you. You did an amazing thing back there at Simon's. I wish you could have seen Simon's face as he heard you talking about him. He looks up to you so much, even after all that's happened. Maybe especially because of all that's happened."

"Then why on earth hasn't the guy called me? Texted? Anything."

Heather's laugh was sweet to hear. "They grounded him from his cell phone and computer outside of classwork until the end of the month."

"Ouch. He said they wouldn't be that cruel."

"I had another visitor this morning, too. What exactly did you say to Candace Norden?"

Max had hoped his role in that one wouldn't ever get back to Heather. She might consider it meddling if not outright manipulation. "Um…about what?"

"She came in asking for the form needed to take a non-student to the homecoming dance. Something about a bargain of a date for an A in algebra? And the chance to put something right?"

Max laughed and slapped his hands over his eyes. "I didn't really think she'd do it." That wasn't exactly true—he'd carefully couched it as an offhand comment, then prayed like crazy that that the notion would stick.

"So you *did* give her the idea to take Simon to homecoming?"

Max winced. He still couldn't read from her tone whether Heather approved or disapproved of his plan, and things were precarious enough between them as it was. "Maybe."

"You convinced a junior on the cheerleading squad to take a freshman in a wheelchair to the homecoming dance?" Was that awe or annoyance?

"Well, okay, there may have been a little incentive thrown in about my paying for dinner at The

Black Swan. They need another chance to get the ramp right, you know."

There was an exasperating silence on the other end of the phone before she replied, "You're amazing."

"Is that amazing great or amazing bad?"

He wouldn't have thought he could hear a smile over the phone, but she sighed in a way that made his heart gallop in his chest. "That's amazing amazing." Her tone required no other qualifier. Max felt his eyes shut and his shoulders unwind. He hadn't lost her. At least not completely. And she didn't know what was coming.

I've gotta win her back, Lord. You know that. I can't lose her. Not yet. Max thought about the package in the back of his van, newly fetched from Violet Sharpton, who was "amazing amazing" in her own right. He checked his watch. Ten after three meant school was done for the day. "Can you meet me at the wheel bridge in half an hour?"

"The wheel bridge?"

"Well, for you it's the footbridge, but you know what I mean." It felt delightful to be able to tease her again. Her laugh untied the knots that had been twisting in his gut for days.

"Do you ever stop, Max?"

Max looked up to see Alex holding up a note in the palm of his hand that read, "Leave now and go get her!"

"Only when there's a staircase, and maybe not even then," he told Heather.

Heather couldn't wipe the smile off her face as she drove past The Black Swan. She'd avoided the place since that night, unable to bear the reminder of how things had unraveled since then. Inside that restaurant, even despite the challenges of making that evening work, Heather had begun to believe she could build a life with Max Jones. It had been an unsteady, fragile belief, but Max's eyes, his passion for life right down to the spontaneous pirouette under the balcony, and his heart-stopping kiss had all bloomed a strength within her.

His actions afterward had put that strength to the test. She knew Max could be bitter and resentful; she'd seen his impulsive side run off with his good sense. Heather didn't want to be caught in the crosshairs of that kind of life, battling someone always on the defensive, always with something to prove. That kind of man had soured her parents' marriage, had tainted her engagement with a man who insisted that God had wronged him.

What she'd heard from Simon's kitchen was a different man. A man who could endure what life—what God—had asked of him. She had always suspected the Max on wheels had become a better man than the Max who walked. The words she'd heard at Simon's house had proven that to be true. As Heather pulled up to the parking lot that sat next to the Gordon River, she knew she was almost ready to give her heart to Max Jones. Almost. She prayed that when she looked into his eyes today, God would grant her whatever last piece she needed to get past "almost."

He sat at the near end of the charming footbridge that was the unofficial symbol of Gordon Falls, a spectacular smile lighting up his face. That grin was accompanied by a twinkle in his eye that couldn't be classified as anything short of mischievous. Max was up to something.

Max was *always* up to something. It was one of the best and scariest things about that man.

"Hi there." The way he looked at her made her feel, well, beautiful. Not glamorous beautiful, but the inner, lasting kind of beautiful. A woman no longer afraid to be noticed. A woman capable of making a difference in someone's life—and not just Simon's and Max's.

"Hello."

She noticed a package in his lap. He caught her gaze and winked. "I'm hoping we have a lot to celebrate today."

Me, too, Heather thought as they moved toward the set of benches that sat at the very center of the bridge, one of the prettiest spots in town. "I'm so glad about Simon."

"That kid's gotten to me. I want him to succeed so

bad I can taste it." He gestured for her to sit down. He was uncharacteristically fidgety, a departure from the ever-cool guy who had rolled up to school back in August. He seemed to know, as she did, that today would be a turning point for them.

"I know you do. I think it's wonderful. And he'll make it. I just know he will."

Max reached out his hand, palm up, asking for Heather's to slip inside his grasp. "I want us to make it, too. I hope you know that. I'm scared to death we don't know how, but if God caught me when I was falling then, I figure he'll catch me when I'm falling now." He wrapped his hand around hers. "I've fallen for you." He suddenly slumped forward, a wincing sort of laugh echoing from up under his shaggy hair. "Oh, man," he moaned, still gripping her hand. "That sounded *so much less stupid* in my head." He looked up at her, cringing and smiling at the same time.

Heather could feel a smile bursting across her face. Max's awkward, imperfect declaration charmed her more than any sonnet or grand gesture. Laugher bubbled up from a joyful place inside her, a place she hadn't felt for a long, long time. "It was…was…" She groped for the right words, settling on, "Wonderfully cheesy."

She pulled his hand to her lips and kissed it. "I fell, too. And I want us to make it, too." She held his callused fingers to her cheek, reveling in the strength of them. "I'm ready, I think. I'm not going to walk away, Max. You need to know that. I don't think I can anymore. I need you too much. I think we need each other." She took a deep breath, daring herself to say what she'd already realized she came there to say. "I'm in love with you. Warts and all, wheels and all, wild and all." Some part of her was so proud to say it first. It was such an enormous leap toward the woman she wanted to be. The woman Max could help her become.

Max reached out to cradle her face in both of his hands. "I am head over wheels in love with you, Heather Browning." With that he kissed her so grandly she nearly fell off the bench, sending them into peals of splendid, happy laughter. "Oh!" he cried, smiling wider than she'd ever seen him. "I can't believe I forgot this. I was going to give this to you before my little speech…." He put his hand to his forehead and moaned, "That horrible little speech. I should have had Alex write me something."

"No," she refuted. "It was perfect. I wouldn't change a word."

Max gave her an I-doubt-that look, but he handed her the package.

Heather saw fringe first. A band of long green fringe, interspersed with a few shots of black. As she began to unfold the soft fluffy fabric, she recognized it as knitting. Only it didn't look like any of the prayer shawls she'd seen before. Opening it more, Heather uncovered an amazing design of the palest pink background with a flock of flamboyant pink flamingos standing on each end. The pattern was such that the fringe looked like sea grass and the black flamingo legs extended down to become the black bits of fringe so that the whole piece looked like two flocks of flamingos standing in the tropics. "Oh, Max! It's incredible!" And it was. It was playful and soft and just a little bit outrageous. The absolute perfect prayer shawl for her. "How?"

"Violet Sharpton. Evidently she enjoys a challenge."

Heather held it up, laughing at the soft and silly flock of her very own. She pulled it around her shoulders, feeling every bit of the affection she knew was behind the gift. "I love it." She leaned over so that the ends found their way around Max's shoulders. "I love you."

Max pulled her down onto his chair. "I was hoping you'd say that." He kissed her again, and they sat there, wrapped up in flamingos and pure joy, looking out at the fall spectacle that was the Gordon River in October.

It was as close to a perfect moment as Heather could ever hope to come. "So I guess we do have a lot to celebrate today," she whispered into Max's hair.

"We could have a whole pie each and not come

close to hitting the mark." Max laughed and planted a kiss on her shoulder.

"I think a slice will do. Karl's?"

He spun the chair in the direction of the riverbank. "Hang on, darlin'—it's all downhill from here."

Heather held up the shawl, letting the fringe flutter in the breeze as they rolled toward town.

Chapter Twenty-Three

Heather still hadn't stopped grinning as she watched Karl push open the back door to let them into the coffee shop. The old man's eyes held a knowing sparkle, making Heather wonder if she and Max looked as obvious as some of the high school's more love-struck couples.

She was not prepared for the waves of applause that broke out as they rolled to the front. She'd forgotten that Karl's gave an unobstructed view of the footbridge. When she saw Violet Sharpton rise from the booth with the best view, she suspected it wasn't a coincidence.

Violet winked and gave Max's shoulder a nudge. "I guess it did the trick?"

Max puffed up his chest. "Well, now, I'd like to think I had the lady's heart before I pulled out the knitting—but it sure helped seal the deal."

Heather gave Violet a hug. "It's wonderful. I can't believe you came up with this design. I love it."

"It was a pleasure to make one for a happy occasion. Or one to *make* a happy occasion. When Max called and asked if it was ready, I knew it was time to get the Tuesday women's prayer chain fired up to help untangle this whole mess. Marge was here having coffee when she caught sight of you two out on the bridge, so she called me." The older woman's eyes sparkled. "Happiest stakeout I've done in a long, long time."

"Thank you, Violet." Max grasped her hand. "Really."

Violet pinched Max's cheek as if he'd just become her eleventh grandchild. "My pleasure, Hot Wheels."

"I may just have to learn to knit this summer when school's out," Heather offered.

"Why wait? Melba's a great teacher, and we could use a few more of your age anyhow." Violet raised an eyebrow at Max. "What about you? You could give knitting a whole new kind of style."

Heather pictured Max with yarn and needles and burst out laughing just as Max vigorously shook his head. "I'll pass," he said. "I'm not ready for that kind of adventure." He took Heather's hand. "If you don't mind, I've got some celebratory pie to eat. And thanks again. You're one awesome grandma."

Violet preened. "One awesome grandma. Maybe I can figure out a way to get that on my license plate like you do. Go on, hon. Go eat pie with your sweetheart."

Heather felt as if her cheeks were burning as she sat at the table Karl had already cleared for Max. The whole restaurant was watching them. Max would always draw attention wherever he went. Was she ready for that? Could she ever grow accustomed to standing out like this with him? He took her hand across the table, his expression warm and encouraging as if he could read her worries. He nodded toward their audience, who were peering over menus or casting glances over coffee mugs or even flat-out staring. "Maybe I could learn not to stand out quite so much, huh?"

She shook her head. "You?"

He gave her a heart-melting look. "I'd do it. For you."

Goodness, but the man could ooze charm. "Don't change. Don't you dare fade into the background."

A little boy walked up to the table and pointed to Max's wheels. "Are you a Transformer? Like on TV?"

His mom immediately planted her hands over the boy's mouth. "I'm so sorry."

"Nah," Max said, smiling. "It's okay, really." He angled out from under the table. "I'm just a guy like you, only my legs don't work as well as yours, so they need a little help. But I can do a few neat tricks." Max shifted his feet to make room on the footrest, the same as he had done for Heather that night. "Here—hop on for a second and I'll show you."

The boy looked up at his mom, who gave a cautious nod. "It'll be fine," Heather added, seeing the mom's worry. "I've done it."

Max told the boy where to hold on, then wheeled out into the aisle and did a series of spins that sent the little guy into a torrent of happy giggles. *He has such a gift for this,* Heather thought. How good it was to admire Max as much as she loved him.

"I can ride bikes like you." Max's voice held a tenderness she hadn't seen in him before. She remembered the hurt in his eyes when the little girl had stared the last time they were in Karl's. That edge was gone. "I like ice cream the same as you, and I have favorite TV shows just like you. We're the same in more ways than we're different. Don't you think?"

"'Cept you gots a girlfriend. I'm too young for that."

Max stared at Heather, holding her gaze with nothing short of a smolder as he spun the boy one last time. "I sure do. And don't worry, I'm sure you'll get your chance one day with a smile like you've got. Hey, what's your name, sport?"

"Theo."

"You go to school here, Theo?"

Theo nodded. "Yep."

"Well, maybe I can come to your class one of these days and show you all my cool wheel toys. Would you like that?"

Heather's heart swelled when Theo's eyes lit up. "Sure!"

"I've got another friend named Simon who is in a wheelchair, too. Okay if he comes along?"

The vision of Max and Simon visiting a kindergarten classroom practically reduced Heather to tears. She grabbed Max's hand as he returned to the table. "Don't you dare change. Don't you dare tone it down, ever." She swiped a tear from her burning cheek. "It's one of the things I love about you."

Max laced his fingers through hers. "*Things? Plural? Good. Let's get some pie and you can tell me all of them.*"

Epilogue

"Why are we stopping at the firehouse?" Heather asked as JJ pulled into the station driveway after they'd had lunch after church one Sunday afternoon.

JJ undid her seat belt. "Max texted and I told him I'd swing by and drop you off."

The February day was unseasonably warm, and Max had made plans to shoot hoops with some of the firemen off shift. The game they played wasn't quite basketball, but some sort of game they'd dreamed up to accommodate Max's sitting versus their standing. He'd explained it to her twice and she'd even sat and watched the day Simon joined in, but she still didn't get it. It didn't really matter—it was fun and Max had developed deeper friendships with several of the GFVFD force. Max's Element in the corner of the drive now boasted an I Support GFVFD sticker on his back window like nearly every other car in town.

She knew the basketball hoop was out back, but that didn't explain why the bay was empty. Usually there was always someone cleaning trucks or washing equipment, but no one could be seen.

"They're probably in there somewhere. Let's go find them."

Heather and JJ pushed through the station doors, Heather wondering if they always kept the lights off like this. Wasn't there supposed to be someone on-site all the time? "Max?" Heather called. "Are you in here?"

"Back here." Max's voice came from the dining room, but she still saw no lights on from over that way.

JJ began flicking light switches as they went until she finally reached the doorway and threw the switch that bathed the dining hall in light.

Revealing Max amid a dozen or so firefighters standing at attention in full dress uniforms behind him.

"Down!" came Chief Bradens's command as he stood directly behind Max.

In perfect unison, the entire department removed their hats and got down on one knee. Heather grabbed the chair next to her for support.

"Since I lack the ability to do this the traditional way, I thought I'd make do with a few extra resources."

He moved toward Heather just as JJ removed

Heather's hand from the chair and guided her down to sit in it.

"Max…"

"Hang on," Max interrupted, his smile a mile wide and a bit nervous at the same time. "You'll get your turn in a minute." He reached behind him on the chair and produced a small black velvet box.

Heather tried to remember how breathing worked and Max moved up right next to her, picking up her left hand and smiling at the fact that she was shaking like a leaf.

"Heather Browning, I'd like very much to spend my life with you. Will you marry me?"

Her powers of speech left the building. She nodded once, then several times, finally choking out a "Yes!" that sent the firemen into thunderous applause and hoots of victory.

Suddenly, more faces appeared from out of the kitchen. Alex smiled and whooped as loud as the firemen. Melba—now fully showing with baby Maria—ran over to give Heather a hug. Heather's mom came out of the kitchen already in full cry mode. Max's mother kissed her son and then kissed Heather, too. Within seconds the room was filled with people she knew and loved—half of Gordon Falls had been in on this, it seemed. Simon—entering his second month back at school—was there, as were his parents. Margot, Violet, Pastor Allen and even Karl.

Tonight, she didn't find she minded being the center of attention at all. Not with Max at her side, not even when Jesse Sykes began crooning the Motown song "Me and Mrs. Jones," earning him a cuff from JJ.

"We've gotta get that boy a girl," Clark Bradens moaned.

"I'm working on it," Melba replied. "He's a bit… outlandish, you know?"

"Sometimes," Heather offered, "those are the very best men of all."

* * * * *

Dear Reader,

Max hounded me until I gave him his own story. This is one of the great experiences for writers—when a story chases you relentlessly until you give it life. The minute Max showed up in *The Firefighter's Match* (Gordon Falls, book 3), I knew he'd never settle for his role as a secondary character. What fun it was to give him a love like Heather Browning! I hope the delight I had in writing this tale comes through for you, dear reader. If this is your first visit to Gordon Falls, make sure you go back and find *Falling for the Fireman* (book 1) and *The Fireman's Homecoming* (book 2), as well as *The Firefighter's Match* (book 3). If you want to know more about the prayer shawl ministry, please email me at allie@alliepleiter.com. As always, you can reach me at my website, www.alliepleiter.com, on Facebook at www.facebook.com/pages/Allie-Pleiter/97112313209, on Twitter at twitter.com/alliepleiter or P.O. Box 7026, Villa Park, IL 60181—I love to hear from you!

Questions for Discussion

1. Have you had your life turned upside down by a tragedy? What have you brought away from that experience?

2. Do you agree or disagree with how Simon's parents are handling his entry into high school?

3. Is there a gathering place like Karl's Koffee in your community? What do you like about it? What don't you like about it?

4. Max escapes on the *Sea Legs*. Where and how do you escape?

5. Have you ever been to a "happy funeral"? How does faith make such a thing possible?

6. Do you know anyone with Max's in-your-face personality? What's good about it? What's not so good?

7. Is there someone in your high school memories who cared about you as much as Heather cares about Simon? What did they add to your life at that time?

8. Max says "the timing is way off" in his relationship with Heather. Have you had a relationship where the timing was "way off"? What happened?

9. If Simon had shown up angry on your doorstep, what would you have done?

10. School bullies are a complex problem to solve. What has been your experience? What's worked? What hasn't?

11. Do you have a Violet Sharpton in your community? What's she (or he) like? What gifts do they bring?

12. How has faith helped you overcome the present and past obstacles in your life?

LARGER-PRINT BOOKS!

GET 2 FREE
LARGER-PRINT NOVELS
PLUS 2 FREE
MYSTERY GIFTS

Love Inspired®
SUSPENSE
RIVETING INSPIRATIONAL ROMANCE

Larger-print novels are now available...

YES! Please send me 2 FREE LARGER-PRINT Love Inspired® Suspense novels and my 2 FREE mystery gifts (gifts are worth about $10). After receiving them, if I don't wish to receive any more books, I can return the shipping statement marked "cancel." If I don't cancel, I will receive 4 brand new novels every month and be billed just $5.24 per book in the U.S. or $5.74 per book in Canada. That's a savings of at least 23% off the cover price. It's quite a bargain! Shipping and handling is just 50¢ per book in the U.S. and 75¢ per book in Canada.* I understand that accepting the 2 free books and gifts places me under no obligation to buy anything. I can always return a shipment and cancel at any time. Even if I never buy another book, the two free books and gifts are mine to keep forever.

110/310 IDN F5CC

Name	(PLEASE PRINT)	
Address		Apt. #
City	State/Prov.	Zip/Postal Code

Signature (if under 18, a parent or guardian must sign)

Mail to the Harlequin® Reader Service:
IN U.S.A.: P.O. Box 1867, Buffalo, NY 14240-1867
IN CANADA: P.O. Box 609, Fort Erie, Ontario L2A 5X3

**Are you a current subscriber to Love Inspired Suspense books and want to receive the larger-print edition?
Call 1-800-873-8635 or visit www.ReaderService.com.**

* Terms and prices subject to change without notice. Prices do not include applicable taxes. Sales tax applicable in N.Y. Canadian residents will be charged applicable taxes. Offer not valid in Quebec. This offer is limited to one order per household. Not valid for current subscribers to Love Inspired Suspense larger-print books. All orders subject to credit approval. Credit or debit balances in a customer's account(s) may be offset by any other outstanding balance owed by or to the customer. Please allow 4 to 6 weeks for delivery. Offer available while quantities last.

Your Privacy—The Harlequin® Reader Service is committed to protecting your privacy. Our Privacy Policy is available online at www.ReaderService.com or upon request from the Harlequin Reader Service.

We make a portion of our mailing list available to reputable third parties that offer products we believe may interest you. If you prefer that we not exchange your name with third parties, or if you wish to clarify or modify your communication preferences, please visit us at www.ReaderService.com/consumerchoice or write to us at Harlequin Reader Service Preference Service, P.O. Box 9062, Buffalo, NY 14269. Include your complete name and address.

LISLPDIR13R